DAYDREAMS

▼

Linda Amnawah

DAYDREAMS

Orders or requests for donations should be addressed to :
The Astoria House/Linda Amnawah
48-08 30th Avenue
P.O. 9072
Astoria, New York 11103
Tel; 718-274-4185

iUniverse books may be ordered through booksellers or by contacting:
iUniverse
1663 Liberty Drive
Bloomington, IN 47403
www.iuniverse.com
844-349-9409

ISBN: 978-0-5951-7666-3 (sc)
ISBN: 978-1-4697-9681-9 (e)

Print information available on the last page.

iUniverse rev. date: 08/03/2023

This book is dedicated to my three children Sarah, Somah, and Joseph and to anyone who took the time to read my book.

Contents

Introduction

This is my book. I wrote it for you. I wrote it for everyone who wants to read it. This is my story which I lovingly composed. Daydreams is about four Puerto Rican girls who are born and raised in New York. The reader gets to share their joys, sorrows, triumphs, and challenges as they grow into mature women.

My objective in writing this novel is to portray a positive image of the Hispanic women. All my life, I had to contend with a preconceived derogatory stereotype. Hispanic women were often associated with welfare, drugs, teenaged pregnancies, and illegitimate children. In this book, I wish to show that there are hardworking, intelligent Hispanics who overcome hindrances without becoming addicted to narcotics or liquor.

Daydreams is a fictional novel. I have created all the characters and circumstances. But I feel that any work of literature is a part of its author's life. We write, as we speak, from our experiences. Every writer looks at his own soul before he puts his words on paper. That's what I did.

I have written a novel about four young Puerto Ricans who met in the first grade at age. As the years went by, their lives became more and more intertwined. Finally, they realized that they had always been there for each other and that they always would. Their biggest and most important asset was their friendship.

That's what my book is about. I hope you enjoy it. I wish to thank my mother, my husband, my children, (Sarah, Somah, and Joseph) for their faith in me. I wish to thank everyone who was ever kind to me. You made my life brighter.

Love,
Linda Prado Amnawah

The Background

The Characters:

Maria Abate-Puerto Rican and Italian-growing up mostly with Mom's family, religious

Amanda Martinez-Puerto Rican and dark skinned, bright, and self conscious

Elaine Rivera-Puerto Rican, very light skinned, and not very bright Carmen Cortez-Puerto Rican, very bright, and determined

Chapter One

Memories

It was a large penthouse overlooking Central Park. Spring was just beginning, and the leaves were a pale green. Schoolchildren could be heard chattering and playing down on the sidewalks. The housekeeper served the "cafe con leche". The four middle aged women sat around a marble coffee table. No one knew exactly what to say. No one wanted to start. All were dying of curiosity.

Finally, the hostess, the olive toned, Amanda, said: "I am so glad you could all come. It is so nice to see you all again (in slightly accented English). I can't tell you how happy I am that you are all here. Smiles broke out from all, even the housekeeper.

Everyone started talking at the same time. Suddenly, everyone wanted to talk and express their felicity at being together again. Everyone felt at home if not in a penthouse but in their association. The warmth they felt for each other united them. The memories flowed.

Setting: Memories
Bergen Street between Smith Street and Hoyt Street. The brownstones had long been abandoned by the former Irish and Italian residents. The buildings on the block was occupied by mostly Puerto Rican families.

The neighborhood was ethnically homogeneous and socio-economical mixed.

There were families who relied on public assistance, there were families in which the parents held civil service jobs, and there were families who owned their own businesses and had vacation homes in Puerto Rico and Connecticut. Still, there was a common bond. They were all Puerto Rican. They didn't all look alike, and they didn't agree on everything, especially political issues, but they all loved their homeland and were proud of their heritage.

The unusual aspect of Bergen Street is that it was a poor neighborhood on the periphery of a very opulent neighborhood-Brooklyn Heights. The reason why the Puerto Rican people who were not poor lived there was because they couldn't rent or buy homes in white neighborhoods. Being Puerto Rican in the late 1950s was not an advantage. These were the days before political correctness and fair housing laws.

The street consisted of very ageing brownstones that were once quite elegant. Some of the more expensive ones had all private rooms; the less costly ones were mostly railroad apartments. All had private bathrooms, which was a source of pride to their residents. There were buildings on other streets in which three or four families on the floor shared a bathroom.

Perpendicular to Bergen Street was Smith Street. Smith Street was where all the shops were. Anything a person wanted could be purchased there. There were several different "bodegas" or grocery stores. Although they carried some of the same products, some of the stores were strikingly dissimilar. There were stores that sold only tropical products from back home and catered basically only to Hispanic customers and people interested in Hispanic products. There were stores that were more Americanized and carried products popular in the United States such as Savarin and Maxwell House coffee and Del Monte canned fruits and fruit juices. Then were stores that sold household items such as "calderos" heavy aluminum pots used to make rice and stews, cutlery, scented candles, coffee pots, and tablecloths as well as foods. Smith Street was always lively. There were always people out even in the wee hours of the night.

It was not politically correct to be half anything and half anything else. But Maria Abate knew which was the better half and identified with it.

Maria was of a Puerto Rican mother and Italian father. But she lived in a Puerto Rican neighborhood. Despite her deep love and closeness to her father, she barely identified with her Italian heritage. Her mother, Angelica Rios, was a very strong woman. Born in the farmlands of Arecibo, Puerto Rico, she went to school up to the eighth grade. Her parents felt that that was all the schooling a girl needed. However, in those days the schools of Puerto Rico required that all children take English as a second language from the first grade on. Therefore, Angelica could read and write English when she came to New York. She spoke with a distinctive accent even after having spent over twenty years here. Angelica came to New York with her mother and five older brothers when her father died in Puerto Rico. She had had eleven brothers but four died in World War II and two chose to stay in Puerto Rico working the family's farm which they divided between the two of them.

Angelica did not marry young like so many of the women from her country. She wanted to work—a radical idea for a Hispanic woman in the 1930s! She took sewing classes at night while she worked in the Ronzoni macaroni factory during the day. Angelica's Mom also needed the money at that time. Eventually, she became a competent dressmaker. She went to work in New York's garment industry in Manhattan.

Angelica was a religious, God-fearing, young woman. She went to work and came right home. She never used cosmetics, and she wore modest clothing. Her skirts were long, and her plain blouses had long sleeves. She attended church on Sundays and participated in church activities. Those were her only form of entertainment. Within the Puerto Rican community in New York in the later 1930s, Angelica was considered a rarity. Some women gossiped about her behind her back. Some tried getting dates for the "poor, lonely, Angelica". What the other young women of the community did not understand was that Angelica was very content with her quiet lifestyle. She ignored the gossip. She never harbored any ill will towards anyone, even her most ardent tormentors.

Angelica was a perfectionist. She always did her best and did not tolerate mediocrity, especially in herself. When she made a dress, every stitch had to be in line even when she knew the boss wouldn't notice. She felt that her work was a direct reflection on herself. Angelica became known as one of the best dressmakers in her factory. She was often chosen to train new workers; a chore she carried out with love. She was revered by the younger seamstresses and envied by the older and less efficient ones. Angelica never minded the negative tones because she felt that she worked for God first and foremost.

One of the few luxuries that Angelica allowed herself was going to the movies. She surely loved the American cinema especially the romantic epics of Clark Gable. She also loved the Westerns featuring John Wayne, Randolph Scott, and Alan Ladd. It was not proper for a young woman to go out alone at night in those days. Therefore, a group of ladies who were not married often went together. The married ones had to stay home and take care of their husbands and children. One Friday night, in late October, Angelica, a distant cousin named Mercedes, and another woman named Jenny got together to go see a John Wayne flick near their homes. On their way home, they stopped for an ice cream soda.

A young man named, Estefano Abate, was working the night shift at the drug store. He waited on them and filled their orders immediately. He had big brown eyes and wavy light brown hair. He spoke Spanish like a native speaker even though he was Italian. He was born in Milan and came to the United States because of political problems at home and problems with his own family. He joined the American army to gain citizenship. He worked as a long shore man but worked in this restaurant when he was laid off from the docks. Angelica thought she'd never fall in love. She thought she'd live with her mother all her life. One look at this exotic young man and her heart skipped a beat. Her life would never be the same. Angelica started looking forward to the Friday night movies and the visits to the ice cream parlor. As a matter of fact, these became the center of her life.

She and Estefano made it a point to not look at each other too much. That's what people did back then when they really liked each other. One Friday evening, near Christmas time, Angelica, Mercedes, and Jenny arrived at the ice cream parlor although it was much too cold for ice cream that day. Almost as soon as they sat down at their usual table, Angelica felt a sensation of utter dismay. Another waiter was standing by their table smiling, asking for their orders. Estefano, he explained, had gone back to work in the docks. The money was much better there and that was his usual occupation anyway. Angelica ordered black coffee. This beverage matched her present mood. The gaiety had gone out of her heart.

Angelica went to work each day and worked her heart out. She became quieter than usual. She ate her lunch by herself. On Sundays, she went to church. After the Mass, she participated in any church activity. She officiated at rummage sales and cake sales to help the parish. She tried to keep her mind off the young man whom she had not had the courage to speak to. At night she read the Spanish language newspapers first to find out what was going on back home and then the English language newspapers to find out what was important in her new country. She felt alone even when surrounded by friends and relatives. The days were unfulfilled, and the nights were lonely. There was nothing to look forward to. Then one day, as if God had answered her prayer, Estefano showed up at her job in Manhattan's garment center. Angelica looked up and saw him talking to the foreman. She thought she was seeing things; she couldn't believe her eyes. It didn't make sense. The foreman pointed her out, and he started walking towards where she was working at her machine. It seemed that he had asked around to find out where she worked. At first, no one seemed to know. Then he ran into Mercedes when he was picking up a final paycheck at the ice cream parlor. She hesitantly told him where Angelica worked. Under protests from both families, Angelica and Estefano were married a year later in St. Agatha Catholic Church. Their bicultural marriage lasted many years and produced one child-a girl, Maria, named after Estefano's mother.

It was 1952 in Brooklyn, a borough of immigrants, but immigrants unlike the Puerto Ricans who were citizens. Although American citizens, the people of Puerto Rico were treated like foreigners and discriminated against as "non-white" wherever they went in the United States. This was especially true for those who looked like they were part Indian or Black. The light skinned ones, who could pass for white fared somewhat better, until at least they disclosed that they were Puerto Rican. Well, at least that's the way it seemed. They were stuck together in their neighborhoods. No matter where they worked, it was always so good to come home to their "barrios". Still, some people did quite well-getting civil service jobs and buying their little houses. Others had it harder.

Lourdes Rodriguez came to New York having finished high school. She had taken a commercial course in her local high school back home. In the late 1940s, there were very few Puerto Ricans in New York and even less Hispanics. Most people were unaccustomed to seeing them and treated them with disdain. Lourdes was tall, slender, and bronze. The latter aspect and her Spanish accented English kept her from getting good jobs in offices. Tired, discouraged, and demoralized, she took a course in sewing and landed a job in New York's garment center. The work was hard, and the hours were long, but the money was good at the time. Dressmakers used to make more than teachers in the late 1940s and early 1950s. Of course, that changed with the exportation of work to foreign countries such as China, Indonesia, Korea, and some of the European countries. The day Lourdes entered the factory, she was pleasantly surprised to see one of her neighbors, that quiet religious, Angelica Rios (soon to be Angelica Abate). They became friends instantly. They had lunch together every day and Angelica taught her how to sew quickly and accurately.

There was someone else at the factory. A handsome truck driver named Miguel Martinez. He was also tall and brown. When he walked in with the new supply of materials, all the Hispanic women turned their heads.

However, he did not seem to bother with the ones who glared at him. He looked at the one who pretended she didn't notice.

Lourdes worked steadily and saved her money. Angelica married Estefano and invited all the "girls" from the factory to the wedding. Miguel, of course, was also invited. He and Lourdes danced almost every dance together. Since the day of Angelica's wedding, they kept company. A year later, Angelica and Estefano danced all night at Lourdes and Miguel's wedding. They also had a daughter, about three months younger than Angelica's daughter. They named her Amanda. She was as dark as Maria was light. The parents did not know that their lives would be parallel for-ever.

The Gowanus housing project had been built in the mid1950s for poor people. Most people who were found eligible for apartments there were either on welfare or held very low paying jobs. The Abate family and the Martinez family would not to be able to live there because of their incomes. Their incomes were not high by the national standards, but they did not fall below the "poverty" lines. The Abates and the Martinez' families were the working poor.

Public housing projects were big miserable looking buildings which were built to house as many families as possible. Some are as high as twenty floors. Adding insult to injury, these cold wretched structures were usually built within the poorest and most dangerous neighborhoods. There were, however, exceptions. The Rivera family lamented living in the Gowanus projects. Their apartment was on the seventh floor. The buildings were always noisy. Teenagers ran around unsupervised. Youngsters were attacked in the elevators and their money, books, and even sneakers were often stolen at knife point. Miranda longed for the sunshine and palm trees of Puerto Rico. Santurce was so beautiful. No public housing projects there. At least not for her. Guillermo, her husband, had made the decision to come to New York. He dreamt of riches and opportunities on the "mainland". Miranda and Guillermo had five children. Guillermo Jr., Miranda, Jesus, Carlos, and Elaine, the youngest. It was hard to earn a living in Puerto Rico, but it was hard to earn a living here too. Guillermo thought that there would be more opportunities for the children here. There was a public school system that was free, and the city college system was free for qualified students.

To their credit, the Rivera children were all bright and hard working. Elaine just seemed a little slower than the others. Miranda wondered if they had done the right thing. Guillermo drove a yellow cab. He worked twelve hours a day for forty per cent of the meter plus tips. Some people gave tips, and some didn't. It was the customer's decision. But what a way to support five children! No wonder they "qualified" for an apartment in the projects. Miranda felt that they had traded their easy-going way of life on their luscious island for a yellow cab and public housing. The Rivera family could not afford private housing at this time, so they did the best they could with what they had. Miranda longed for better times. She and Guillermo often quarreled about whether to go back home or stay here. For Miranda, the decision would be easy; for Guillermo it was hard. So, they stayed. Guillermo driving twelve hours a day and Miranda taking care of five children in a public housing project in which she could not let the children go out to play by themselves.

This South Brooklyn neighborhood was made up of mostly working people. They were the majority. They were the people who kept New York City running—the dressmakers, dock workers, cooks, waiters, waitresses, house keepers, maintenance, and construction workers. These people are the unnoticed, silent mass of humanity without which this city could not progress and succeed.

While it is true that many live in cold and unkempt apartment buildings, there were some who rose above the others. Such was the Cortez family. Fernando Cortez was from a proud and prosperous family in Rio Piedras, Puerto Rico. He had never lived in the countryside known affectionately as "El Campo". His father worked as a bookkeeper in Puerto Rico and his mother taught school in San Juan. They were middle class and had always been. Fernando was a tall, sandy-haired, man who had blue-gray eyes. His parents had always been good to him. They had provided their son with every material desire. He had never lacked for anything. He had a younger sister named Mercedes. Mercedes was as hard working as Fernando was easy going.

Fernando attended the University of Puerto Rico. He was bright but not terribly diligent. He majored in Psychology and minored in Education. He told his parents that if he did not go on to graduate school to become a psychologist, he could always teach elementary school. That was his backup plan. It's a good thing for Fernando that he had a backup plan.

Fernando, being easy going, decided to take on a job as an elementary school teacher. He taught the fourth grade and coached a baseball team after school. He was well liked by the children, the parents, and the administration. He was young, handsome, and well to do. It seems that there was nothing Fernando was lacking—except maybe a girl to love. Little did he know that he would lose his heart soon enough.

Myra Sierra was a tall, svelte, tan, girl of eighteen years of age. Her people had always worked on the farms, and she knew no other life. The city was a foreign and unknown country to her. She did not finish high school because her father did not see the need to send girls to school. She was the youngest of twelve children. There were older brothers; she was the only girl. However, the small farms faced big competition from the huge sprawling spreads owned by the American corporations. Myra's father was not doing well at all. The nine oldest boys had married and left. They had children of their own already. Myra's father worked on the land with his two youngest sons. Still, times were hard. It was a blessing from God that they could grow food for themselves and that the land they lived on was paid for. There was little of anything else. Myra had never even shopped at a department store in the nearest town. Her mother made all her clothes. Almost all the country girls could sew. Myra's father, Rafael, surely tried. He was in his fields at four o'clock in the morning. He cultivated his land. He fed his animals. He drove his produce to the markets and wrangled out the best prices possible. But with so much competition one could barter just so much.

One day, in early June, the boys were busy on the farm and Myra accompanied her father to the market in Rios Piedras. They sold as much as they could to the wholesalers and then parked the truck on a side street. Fernando Cortez walked lazily towards his home. He had had an especially trying day with the children in the classroom and on the baseball field. It was hot. It is always hot in Puerto Rico but today seemed worse than ever. He walked along and noticed a truck. A large bronze campesino was selling fruit from his truck. A big juicy orange would be great at this time. Maybe they had some fruit juice he could drink on his way home. He decided to check it out.

Suddenly, he saw what looked to him like a goddess. This girl was young. Maybe ten years younger than him. But he knew she was someone he would not forget easily. His blue gray eyes locked with her ebony ones as he approached the truck. He didn't know what he wanted to buy so he told her to give him a pound of everything. He babbled. His words sounded gibberish. He laughed and she smiled back. Her father called her to the truck. He had begun loading what was left of the produce. She walked over and gently began to help. The old truck rambled away taking along Fernando's heart.

He could not sleep that night. He sat up next to the window and thought. He thought and thought. He thought and thought about this girl until his head hurt. The next day, he got up very early because he had not really been sleeping. He taught his class with a rare enthusiasm. That afternoon, he walked the same route looking for the truck. He walked the same route every afternoon looking for the truck. That wagon had to come by sometime.

Six months passed. He looked for and dreamt about the girl he couldn't get out of his mind. He imagined her in all different places. He pretended that they went to dinner together. What would it be like to marry her and have children? What town did she live in? She wasn't from around here. She was a campesina. She came from the farmlands. Fernando was not very familiar with the countryside. His family, as far as he knew, had all been from the city. His family was arrogant in that respect. His parents both looked down on the farmers.

They looked down on anyone who was different from them. Fernando was of direct Spanish dissent. His parents were very proud of their light skin. They boasted of being of Galician origin. Fernando never cared about such things. This young woman who had captured his emotions may be of African and Indian descent. That was fine with him.

One day, Fernando came out of his school during his lunch hour. He went into the bodega across the street and bought pineapple juice in a big paper cup. As he strolled nonchalantly back to his school, there it was. The time worn truck with the fruit and fruit juices. Was the girl there? He ran impulsively in search of his dream. There she was. He looked at her and said: I just bought pineapple juice. I wish I had known you were here I would have bought it from you. At that point, she laughed unceremoniously and asked what she could do.

He said: "Just give me a pound of everything". "And your phone number, I'd really like to get to know you."

Mr. Fernando Cortez and Miss Myra Sierra were married a year later in a small chapel in San Juan. Myra's family attended the wedding. Fernando's friends, colleagues, and some of his students attended. Fernando's parents said that if he married a black campesina he was on his own. Fernando couldn't have been happier.

They moved to New York City to start over. Fernando bought his bride a small two apartment house on Bergen Street with the money he had saved up. He could not teach in New York City because he did not have New York State Certification and his English was not good enough to pass the New York City teacher's certification, but he passed a test for the New York City Post Office and started on a managerial level. His job and the rent from the upstairs apartment would suffice to live decently. The young couple had two children-Fernando Jr. and Carmen.

Chapter Two

Experiences

It was September 1960. The autumn leaves fell delightfully over the brownstones on Bergen Street covering the blue gray sidewalks with their luscious auburn color. SCHOOL STARTED TOMORROW. The mothers were excited, and the children were fearful. Most children had already been warned that they could not speak Spanish in school. They would be taught by teachers who only spoke English.

The Abates were aglow. Maria was going to school for the first time. Angelica had done her best to teach her the alphabet and how to write her name. Estefano had taught her how to add and subtract within ten. Maria knew the names of the colors and the names of some of the geometrical shapes. Maria was going to Catholic school. Angelica had her new plaid uniform and white blouse ready. Maria had brand new black oxford shoes that cost eighteen dollars.

The Martinez family buzzed with excitement. There was a new baby boy who sat up in his crib watching all the adults run around. Because of the recent arrival, Lourdes had not had so much time to plan and to prepare Amanda for school. She had certainly done her best. There was another little mouth to feed, and money was tight. It wasn't the same as when Amanda was the only child. Still, Amanda had a new uniform and shoes. Lourdes thanked God that Catholic schools required uniforms and she would not have to buy new clothes every few months.

Elaine Rivera did not understand why she had to go to Catholic school when all her older siblings had gone to public school. Miranda and Guillermo felt that Elaine, being a little slow, would be treated in a more humane fashion in a religious oriented school. They had never been church going people, but it was not too late to start. They'd do it for their child. The two oldest children were working part time and contributing to the family's finances. Therefore, the few dollars a month for the Catholic school was not a problem. Besides, they' d save money on clothes. Elaine did look darling in her new uniform. The black oxfords were handed down from her sister, but once Guillermo had polished them, they looked as good as new.

Fernando was outraged that the "Friends" school would not accept his children. He had tried to enroll Fernando Jr., the year before. They told Fernando that Fernando, Jr. "did not meet the criteria". Fernando knew that the color of his son's skin kept him out. When it was time for Carmen to attend school, Fernando enrolled her in the same Catholic school as Fernando Jr. He'd be starting the second grade when she'd be starting the first. Myra had gone out and bought Carmen the best shoes available in Abraham and Strauss on Fulton Street and the finest white blouse. The uniform was standard, but Myra had bought two extra jumpers. Fernando worked for his wife and children, and he didn't mind showing it.

Hoyt Street reverberated with the sound of the children and their mothers going to school. The Catholic school students walked south while students attending public school walked north on Hoyt Street. The parents exchanged cold looks as they passed. Each thought that they had taken the right course of action. The Catholic school kids walked in their bright new plaid uniforms. The girls wore plaid jumpers and white blouses, and the boys wore navy blue pants, white shirts, and plaid ties. All the children wore black oxford shoes. The students attending public school wore new, brightly colored clothes. Girls could not wear pants to school at that time.

The neighborhood Catholic school was a mystical old building astoundingly resembling an old castle. No one knew when St. Agatha's had been built. The church beside the school was an exquisite structure that rivaled St. Patrick's Cathedral in Manhattan. Angelica was so proud to have this school and church in her neighborhood. She worshipped there every Sunday and looked forward to her only daughter learning the Catechism in this fine school. Her heart swelled as she reached the school. Maria's heart swelled too but with fear of entering such an exotic-looking building. Most of the other kids on the block were attending the newly built public school closer to home. Why couldn't she go there? The child saw no logic in her parents' decision.

All the first graders and their parents were directed to the auditorium on the third floor. The principal, a sister of St. Joseph, introduced herself and proceeded to call out the names of the children and the class number that they were assigned to. Class 1A was filled with the children who had attended Kindergarten or Day Care and had some skills. Class 1 B was filled with children who had no previous schooling. Maria Abate, Carmen Cortez, Amanda Martinez, and Elaine Rivera were all called in alphabetical order and assigned to Class 1B.

Angelica Abate smiled with delight. Myra and Fernando Cortez shrugged, feeling that their daughter should have been assigned to Class 1 A. Lourdes Martinez was happy that Amanda and Maria Abate were in the same class. Miranda Rivera hoped that Elaine would like school and do well. She hoped the sisters would be considerate of her and make sure that the other children treated her kindly.

The children walked in line down to their classrooms. The mahogany desks were nailed to the floor. The cast iron book holders were below the chairs. There were ink wells embedded in each desk, but no one used ink any- more (especially not in the first grade). The students of class 1B were assigned desks and cubbies to store their coats. Elaine had trouble hanging up her coat, so Carmen helped her. Sister Amarta then assigned them to the same cubby. When she assigned seats, she sat Carmen right behind Elaine.

Maria and Amanda stood close to each other hoping to be assigned that way. The strategy worked. Elaine and Carmen sat in the first row. Maria sat right behind Amanda in the second row. Thus, their lives began to interlock.

The teaching was all in English as expected. The children took out their new notebooks. Each child was asked to say their names round robin style. Maria Abate beamed with delight when she was asked. Elaine stuttered slightly but managed to get both her first name and her last name out. Carmen said hers nonchalantly. Sister Amarta then explained that she would be teaching reading, writing, Mathematics, and Religion. She asked the children if anyone knew what the word "catholic" meant. No one knew.

Afterwards, it was time to give out the books. The girls were awed with their shiny new textbooks. Even though they couldn't read yet, the pictures were lovely. It was so nice to have them. They eagerly turned the pages looking at the brightly colored pictures. There were girls and boys in costly clothes laughing and playing. There were pictures of parks covered in bright green grass, yellow sliding ponds and golden colored swings. This playground surely did not look like the one in the Gowanus housing project. The public park in South Brooklyn had run down, weather beaten, benches in which some of the wood had already fallen off due to decay. The swings were held up by corroded chains which had once been silver, but no one remembers seeing them that way.

Looking at the books, the girls were able to imagine what it would be like to play in a park like that. Their daydream was broken when the teacher asked the class to put the books away. It was time for lunch and Sister Amarta wanted to show the first graders where they would sit for lunch. Each class had its own section. Sister Amarta instructed all the children how to stand by their seats until she called their row. Then they got in a line. Elaine was first in line. She seemed hesitant as she walked to take her place in line, so Carmen prompted her along. Elaine didn't under- stand when Sister Amarta told her in English to hold the door for the class, so Carmen told her softly in Spanish. Amanda and Maria were in the middle of the line. They walked straight and looked ahead. Neither one of them wanted to be caught "talking".

After lunch, there was a half hour recess in the school yard. The first graders wandered around aimlessly because they didn't know anyone. Carmen decided to stay near Elaine because she looked so lost. They talked and walked all around the school yard eager to learn its framework. There was enough time to jump rope and play ball. Carmen said that she would bring her jump rope the next day. Elaine smiled in delight.

The day went quickly. Outside the school, the parents waited anxiously. Angelica had missed a day of work at the garment center to bring Maria to school and pick her up at three o'clock. Lourdes arrived at the corner of Hoyt Street at the same time she did. They laughed and joked about taking the day off. They pondered a solution for the rest of the school year. Neither one really had money for baby-sitters. Myra and Fernando arrived in their new sixties Chevrolet. Other parents glanced through the corners of their eyes not wanting to show that they were looking. All were covetous but none wanted to show it. Miranda hurried out of the projects and onto Hoyt Street. She had just finished serving Guillermo his lunch. He went off in his taxi to complete his shift. Miranda's older children would be coming home soon from the public school, and she was worried.

The parents chatted and exchanged opinions about Catholic school education, the uniforms, and the tuition. Soon the line of first graders appeared. The children walked in two straight lines up to the corner then ran off individually to meet their parents. Carmen introduced her new friend, Elaine, to her parents. Elaine introduced Carmen to her mother. The mothers quickly became acquainted.

Hoyt Street again sang with the voices of school children and their parents. Families walked off in unison. There was magic in the air. This was the first day of school. This was the first day of learning in the new country. This was the first day of learning in their new language.

Although they did not know it at the time, four girls were about to plant flowers in the side roads of each other's lives. The Catholic school children walked north on Hoyt Street while the other children walked south on Hoyt Street. All of them were going home after the first day of what was going to be the experience of a lifetime.

As Carmen and Elaine began to seal their friendship so did their parents. Elaine, although a diligent student, displayed difficulty learning even the most basic tasks. Miranda helped her at home, but Miranda's lack of English skills hampered her efforts to aid her daughter. Elaine's older siblings held after school jobs and had lots of homework of their own. Sometimes, they'd review the alphabet or the numbers with her. One day, over cafe con leche, Miranda shared her concerns with Myra Cortez. Myra suggested that Elaine and Carmen do homework together. Since Miranda had so many children at home, it would be better if Elaine came home with Carmen. Miranda offered to pay. Myra knew she couldn't and pretended that Elaine would be doing Carmen a favor because they could play afterwards. Carmen had no sisters, only a brother, and hadn't made many friends on the block.

June came quickly. Maybe not quick enough for the children but too fast for the parents. St. Agatha's principal, a nun in her late seventies, made all the children pass a rigorous reading test and all their academic subjects before she would approve them for promotion to the next grade. Maria and Amanda, who often did homework and studied together, had no problem passing the test and scholastic courses. Carmen excelled in every area. Elaine, with help from Carmen, her mother, and older siblings, passed with the minimal grade accepted.

St. Agatha's was no picnic academically. But that's precisely why parents made sacrifices to send their children there. The public schools were performatted with problems such as—fights, racial disputes, and subjective teachers who didn't show concern or respect for these new immigrant children.

The children got a good academic education and good religious practice which, the parents hoped, would guide them throughout their entire lives in this parochial school.

Summers in South Brooklyn were something to look forward to. The weather resembled that back home. The public park in the Gowanus projects was an object d' art. During the summer, the girls were free to play there every day if they wanted. The sprinklers provided all the cooling off a child needed. No one needed a store-bought bathing suit—a worn pair of shorts and a tee shirt were just fine. The children of South Brooklyn ran and played together. In the park, there were no Catholic School kids or public-school kids. There were no middle-class kids and no poor kids. All were one.

At first, Carmen's mother was skeptical about letting her play in "that park". It was a ghastly sight compared to the breathtaking parks in Puerto Rico. But this place was their reality now. What alternative was there? Therefore, when Elaine asked Carmen to play outside, Myra reluctantly agreed. She smiled and said a silent prayer.

"I want to ride the swings!" yelled Elaine, as the girls raced down the street.

"OK, I want to ride the swings too," agreed Carmen.

It was easier said than done. The swings were full. Each of the twelve swings were occupied by a child and there were children waiting. The two seven-year-olds moved over to the sliding pond. There they could stand on line and just slide down when it was their turn. There were several children there, but no one could claim ownership. Carmen and Elaine darted towards the slides gleefully enjoying this lightsome day of freedom. They slid down and almost knocked each other off. At the other side of the park, Maria and Amanda frolicked in the in sprinklers. Angelica watched from a distance, not wanting the girls to feel that they were being scrutinized. The girls laughed and ran around splashing water. They wore their old clothes and mostly wore sneakers. This park was nothing like the one in the reader at school but it sure was fun.

Eventually, Carmen and Elaine wandered over to the pool area. They were not dressed properly for the pool, but being seven-year-olds, they threw caution to the winds and ran in. They bolted and raced gleefully into the mild drizzle and into their two classmates and friends. Angelica went home quickly for more towels. Afterwards, she treated all four girls to ice cream from the Mr. Softie truck. The ice cream cones with colored sprinkles sealed a friendship that would be boundless.

School was fun but hanging out in Gowanus Park after school was more fun. The girls grew rapidly. Their parents became friends through them. Maria, Amanda, Carmen, and Elaine became very close friends. Maria was somewhat closer to Amanda because their mothers had been friends. Carmen was a little closer to Elaine because their mothers had known each other first. However, Angelica, Lourdes, Myra, and Miranda, the "Moms" also became friends participating in PTA meetings and playing Bingo at St. Agatha's. The years went by fast.

Finally, they arrived at the eighth grade. The girls had grown physically and emotionally. Their lives had been centered around the church, their community and each other. The girls had no secrets from each other.

Maria often talked about her parents. She was an only child. She had no one to confide in. Although her mother was kind and attentive, Maria felt that there was a big generation gap and did not feel comfortable confiding her fears and her doubts to her mother. Luckily, she did not have to keep them bottled up because she had three helpful friends to talk to.

Maria's life was changing in a subtle manner, and she couldn't explain or understand the change. Her mother looked sad and worried. Her father stayed up at night by the window, sometimes coughing heavily. He barely slept.

"He's home." Amanda assured her. "He's not leaving home." "Maybe he doesn't feel well," added Carmen.

"Your mom knows what she's doing, don't worry." said Elaine.

"If you ever need me, I'm there for you," Amanda assured Maria again.

"Me too," said Carmen and Elaine in unison.

All the girls laughed at this. Still, Estefano started going to work less and less. He was home sick often. Angelica worked longer hours and on Saturdays. Mrs. Ramos, the owner of the bodega, extended credit to the Abate family. They had never been in debt before. Mrs. Ramos was a strict

Pentecost woman who believed that we were placed on this earth to serve humanity and bring others to God. She had known Angelica for many years. She was always leery of her Italian husband, but Angelica was Puerto Rican, and she wasn't going to let her starve. She knew Angelica would pay her bill at the store as best she could. We are all God's children thought Emilia Ramos to herself.

Graduation loomed close at St. Agatha's School. The girls were excited. They didn't feel like studying and doing homework, but they weren't going to flunk out in the last year either. The talk centered around the graduation celebrations each one would have and the dresses they would wear. Amanda and Maria would have dresses made for them by their mothers. Carmen's dress had already been bought at A & S on Fulton Street. Angelica, Maria's Mom, was making Elaine a dress also but Elaine didn't know yet. Angelica and Miranda had made the arrangements to surprise Elaine.

It was a delightful Autumn afternoon in late November and the girls sat on the jerrybuilt benches of the Gowanus Park. They had retired from riding swings and sliding ponds years ago. They parleyed about the boys in their class—the ones they liked and the ones they didn't like. At five o'clock, they started for home. It was an inflexible rule that they had to be home before dark. Elaine lived in the projects, so she only had to go outside the park to her building. The other three walked swiftly to Bergen Street. As they turned the corner, they heard the sirens. Police!

Maria's father dies.

"Oh, God, no!" cried Carmen. "Police on this block!" "Drugs!" yelled Maria. "Did they find someone with drugs?" "I hope it's not Dona Laura's boy" added Maria.

She knew her neighbor's son was always in trouble.

The police car positioned itself in front of Maria's house. As if to keep in tune, an ambulance hurried onto the block right after it. The paramedics ran out of the ambulance and up the stairs. Maria's heart started to beat fast. Tears surged in her eyes. She raced towards her home. She felt faint. It seemed that her legs would give out from under her.

"What has happened?" she asked, speaking to herself. "Let's see, don't cry." comforted Carmen.

"It's probably not for your apartment. What would the police and para-medics be doing in your house?" consoled Amanda.

The three girls dashed towards the venerable brownstone and up the wavering stairs. When they reached the second floor, Angelica stood in front of her door directing the paramedics. Two police officers were already inside. When her mother turned towards her, Maria saw the tears. Mama never cried. Never.

A big policeman came out of the apartment looking sorrowful. He placed his massive hand on Angelica's shoulder and told her he was sorry. Angelica looked straight at the interior of the apartment not turning towards the policeman. The tears streamed silently down her tan cheeks as she tried to fall back on her stoic Christian background. The only man she had ever loved had just passed out of her life—the victim of a massive heart attack. She barely felt Maria's arms around her. Their tears mingled.

At the bottom of the steps, Carmen and Amanda did not know what to say. So, they kept quiet. What could you say to a best friend who just lost her father so abruptly?

The eighth grade sat quietly as they waited for the Abate family to arrive for the funeral mass. They walked subdued after the coffin. Angelica and the Rios family members walked in with several Abate cousins. The Mass started. Amanda, Carmen, and Elaine tried to get Maria's attention, but it was all in vain. She couldn't hear or see them. When the black limousine took the family away to the burial, the girls spoke softly of their friend and her mother. Maria had no sisters or brothers like all of them had. Angelica worked in the garment center. They decided to form an alliance and aid Maria so she wouldn't feel so alone.

Amanda and Maria walked home from school every day but now Maria stayed in Amanda's house until Angelica picked her up. This arrangement worked out well because the girls went to the same school and the women worked in the same factory. Although the sadness that engulfed Maria lingered, the warmth offered by the Martinez family helped to alleviate the pain.

While there was sadness among the residents of Bergen Street and among the children at St. Agatha, there was also zest about the upcoming graduation. It was almost time for the students at St. Agatha's to take the Cooperative examinations. These tests would determine if they'd be able to attend a Catholic high school in the fall. They all anxiously anticipated the coming of the examination.

Maria listened quietly and inattentively as the others discussed their choices of high schools and the scores that they needed to enter. She began to study less and skipped some of the homework assignments. Her mid ninety average was rapidly going down. Estefano was not there to tell her he loved her. He was not there to sign her homework in his fancy handwriting. He was not there to tell her to place herself on a pedestal and reach for the stars. The stars, he used to say, were there for the taking. Well, that wasn't the case anymore, was it? The stars and her father had both left. Making things worse, her mother had never told her that her father had a heart condition. She never knew that he had suffered two mild heart attacks before having the one that took his life.

The girls walked together to St. Joseph's High School the day of the test. They carried with them two "number two" pencils, their school I.D., their admission cards, and a snack. The assay was going to be almost four hours long with a short break. The battery of sub tests seemed easy to Carmen, challenging but fair to Amanda, hard to Elaine and endless to Maria. The first step towards high school was over. Maria didn't care which high school she went to. It just didn't matter. She placed the diocesan high school as her first choice. Maria didn't think that she was going to a parochial high school because she thought her mother would not be able to pay for it.

Carmen's parents wanted her to go to the exclusive Fontbonne Hall in Bay Ridge, but she didn't want to go there. It was all white and she would not be comfortable. Elaine wanted to go to any high school she could get into. Her parents had already assured her they could cover it. Amanda's father had suffered an injury on his truck and had been unable to work. Her parents had already informed her that she could not go to a Catholic school unless Dad's workmen compensation settlement came in. She took the cooperative examination anyway. She hoped her father's workmen's compensation benefits would come in before she started high school. It didn't.

Chapter Three

High School

The sun gleamed brightly on the brownstones of Bergen Street giving them a blessed distinctiveness during September of nineteen sixty-eight. Today was as exhilarating as the first day at St. Agatha's eight years ago. It was the first day of high school. Amanda stood in front of her mirror. She was going to school in street clothes since she was going to her zoned public high school. Sadly, she held acceptances to three Catholic high schools which her parents could not afford. Swallowing her disappointment, she dressed carefully for the occasion. Could she handle a public school after so many years in Catholic school? You bet she could! She wanted to be a doctor, a pediatrician. She wanted it so intensely that nothing was going to stand in her way. This was the first time she'd be in school without her three friends. She would miss Maria the most. Even in her state of melancholy, Maria was still her best friend. Dona Angelica had found a way to send Maria to Catholic school. She used the money from Maria's father's insurance policy. Dona Angelica felt that that's what Estefano would have wanted. Maria would have gladly gone to school with Amanda.

Elaine got into the diocesan Catholic school. She was rejected by all the others. She was placed in what was called the "basic program". Most of the girls in this class took a commercial course and worked after high school.

Elaine was happy because Maria was going to the same school although Maria got into the Honors program. They'd be together in periods like lunch, gym, and assemblies. Maybe they'd be in an Art or Music class together. The Rivera family was overjoyed that Elaine had got- ten approved for the parochial school. All her older siblings agreed to help their parents pay for it.

Carmen's parents decided against the Catholic school system and sent her to the acclaimed private high school in Brooklyn Heights. She didn't want to go. She would have loved to go to the diocesan high school with her best friend, Elaine. She would have even gone to the neighborhood public high school with Amanda. She would have gone anywhere except where her parents were sending her.

Elaine walked out of her building in the Gowanus projects all alone and turned in the direction of Maria Abates' house. Together they took the train into Bensonhurst. Although they had lived in Brooklyn all their lives, neither girl had ever been in this neighborhood. It was an unfamiliar locale to them. It was a white neighborhood also which made the situation more complicated for them.

The school was big and contemporary. They'd miss the antiquated St. Agatha's. As they exited the subway and reached the new high school, they held hands.

Meanwhile, Amanda held back the tears as she waited for the bus. She should be attending the Honors program in any one of the Catholic schools she was accepted to. Instead, she was going to the zone school with students who might be in gangs or on drugs. For a moment, she hated her father for having had an accident and her mother for not earning enough to pay her tuition. But she knew it wasn't their fault. Still, she detested being away from her friends. She worried about Elaine. Maria would probably help her with her homework now. They'd be taking the same type of courses. Carmen was going to private school.

At the same time, Fernando Cortez beamed with pride as he drove his children to private school. Carmen and her brother chortled in the back seat. When was Dad going to understand that he was not high class here.

Why couldn't he stop pretending to be white? If he wanted to be white so bad, why did he marry their mother who was so dark? He knew his children wouldn't be white. Still, they understood that their father meant well. He was raised upper class in Puerto Rico, and it is difficult to change prototypes. Here he was a member of a minority group. Everyone understood that except him.

Back in the neighborhood, Mrs. Ramos' bodega was the place where most people shopped for their daily groceries. Some families even shopped for the week there. The proprietor was an ardent Christian woman who was hardworking and honest. Myra Cortez didn't work, so for her the bodega was a social club and Mrs. Ramos had become just about her best friend. Myra had money of course because of Fernando's salary and the wise investments he had made. However, Myra was often lonely. Mrs. Rivera had so many children and Angelica Abate and Lourdes Martinez worked. Emilia Ramos ran her store almost all by herself. Her husband, Javier, went to the wholesalers and purchased the merchandise. He also made deliveries for one of the wholesalers to earn extra income. The bodega wasn't always so profitable. Business was slow in the late morning. In the early morning, Emilia was busy selling sandwiches and coffee to the people who were going off to work. Things settled down about 10 a.m. That's the time that Myra usually wandered in. They talked about things back home and gossiped about the neighbors. Myra bought everything there just to throw some business Emilia's way. The Ramos' had never had any children of their own. So, they grew very fond of Carmen and Fernando Jr. As a matter of fact, Fernando Jr. worked in the store on weekends. Myra felt this would keep him out of trouble and teach him the value of hard work. Emilia began to feel like she was the "second mother" to the Cortez children. Carmen felt very "at home" when visiting the bodega. Emilia Ramos was a strong independent woman. Carmen admired this woman who ran her own business and held her own in a male dominated world. Emilia Ramos was also a kind and sweet woman who genuinely cared about her friends and neighbors.

Carmen was deeply moved when she heard Mrs. Ramos had extended credit to Maria's Mom when her father was sick. Emilia Ramos was a good person- no question about it. All was good in the neighborhood, but all was not good for Amanda is her high school.

Amanda faces challenges in high school.

Put that back! Amanda thundered at the girl who took money off her tray.

Make me! What are you going to do? retorted the girl in the same tone.

You'll see! You'll see! Amanda bellowed, trying not to look afraid.

Do it then! Do it! The instigator teased.

Amanda was clearly at a loss. St. Agatha had not prepared her for fights in the cafeteria. The other students had gathered around to witness the fight. No one made any attempt to break it up. After what seemed to be an eternity, a teacher appeared. The diminutive Biology teacher took both girls by the arm and led them away. In a corner of the General Office, the teacher, Mrs. Marino, demanded to know the origins of the fracas.

Amanda spoke first. She had purchased her lunch. She put the change on her tray. This other girl walked up to her and impudently took the money. Amanda demanded that she give it back. Mrs. Marino knew that Amanda was telling the truth. The other girl, Martha Williams, was a known agitator who was repeating the ninth grade. As a result of Mrs. Marino's review, Martha was suspended for a week.

Amanda knew that she was in rough terrain and would have other problems. Martha would be back. There would be other rabble rousers, but Amanda now had a new saint. Amanda would forever adore this Science teacher who had come to her rescue. She loved Science and now she would be studying with a teacher she already admired.

Elaine adjusts to her curriculum.

Elaine looked around. She was the only Hispanic student in her class.

She thought that there would be lots of minority group students in the basic program. But because of the zoning law for the Diocesan high school, most of the students were white. Elaine truly felt out of place. Once the books were given out, and the course outline explained, Elaine started to feel better. She knew high school would be harder than junior high school, but the courses looked like they were within her reach.

The Catholic high school had a large modern cafeteria. The tables were small and clean. Staff members washed each table with sterile cloths after each lunch period. Each table had four chairs. Once a student chose a table, she had to sit there each day for lunch. The seats were reserved—more or less. That was good for Maria and Elaine. They ran to each other at lunch the first day and selected a table. Two other girls asked to sit with them—Virginia, who was Puerto Rican and Filipino, and Ann Marie, a girl of Italian heritage. The four girls spent the lunch period getting acquainted. High School wasn't going to be so bad after all.

Carmen adjusts to the private school.

Carmen never felt so out of place in her life. This private school was upper class only because the students had money. Some of them were already displaying terrible manners. They were "snotty"—that is nasty. Carmen longed for her friends—especially Elaine. This school had been her father's decision. He hadn't even consulted her or Fernando Jr. Thank God she could have lunch with her brother who undoubtedly was as uncomfortable as she was. The classes were not going to be very hard. Carmen knew she could handle the curriculum. Carmen had always been a brilliant student. There were no Hispanic students in the entire school except the Cortez'. The high school, however, only had about one hundred and fifty students. Carmen didn't like this place nor would she ever. She knew from the first day.

Gowanus Park Provides Comfort

The autumn leaves fell on the ground of the Gowanus projects covering it with a golden hazel tone. No matter how difficult their adjustment to their new surroundings was, the park always appeared to be a safe refuge. The girls discussed their different experiences. Elaine was distressed at how hard the assignments were. Maria, the always patient friend, helped her as much as she could. Elaine had also signed up for tutoring at the school. Seniors tutored underclassmen for extra credit. Elaine wanted to be a nurse. She wanted to help cure sick people, but the Science courses seemed so difficult. She wondered why she needed so much science when nurses just walked around the hospital taking care of people.

Amanda chuckled quietly at Elaine's reasoning, although she understood what her friend was trying to say. Amanda was having a hard time with the delinquents in the school. Having been raised in a Catholic family and having attended a Catholic school, she never had a fight in school. Now she had that belligerent Martha Williams on her back. Martha was such a coward. She didn't fight one on one. She was always trying to organize a clique of girls to help her fight Amanda. Maria went to school because she had to go. She was still angry and hurt that her mother hadn't told her about her father's heart condition. Maria studied just enough to pass her courses. Carmen disliked her new environment. She loved coming to Gowanus Park every day after school and chatting with her friends. She hoped the years would go fast.

The first year did pass quickly. Elaine passed all the courses in her program. She was in the non-Regents curriculum. The courses were easier than those that Maria was taking. Maria would be getting a Regents diploma if she passed everything. Elaine and her parents were happy that she was graduating from a decent high school with a diploma. The first year had seemed tense but plausible.

Maria became interested in school again—partly because of her friends and partly because of the intervention of a nun named Sister Theresa. She started to study hard in the second semester and her grades improved. She decided to become a teacher and work with children. She wanted to work more with underprivileged children like herself and her best friends. She came to admire many of her teachers especially her Spanish teacher and her Social Studies teacher. Maria came to love and respect her mother again.

Amanda finally beat up Martha Williams at the end of freshmen year. "El que me la hizo, me la pago ". Amanda wasn't going to take it anymore. She cornered Martha one day in the lunchroom and slapped her around when her friends weren't there. All the other girls saw what a bad gutless person Martha really was, and no one was going to be apprehensive of her ever again. Amanda had succeeded in a public school after having attended Catholic schools for years.

She was never going to let herself get pushed around again. Mrs. Marino helped her get into the Honors program in her school. This way she came in earlier and left earlier than the general population and wouldn't have to deal with the troublemakers. Amanda was proud of herself. She always wanted to be a doctor. She decided during her freshmen year that nothing was going to stand in her way. She'd graduate from this school and go to college to study medicine. Mrs. Marino and her parents were there to help her.

Carmen went to school and pretty much kept to herself. She had no desire to mingle with her fellow students. But she came to love the curriculum. The courses were innovative. She didn't have to take final exams; she only had to do a project. She was able to choose the topics in consultation with the teachers. Many of her classes allowed open discussions. She was allowed to have an opinion in her Social Studies classes. These Social Studies classes were divided into courses called Political Science, Sociology, and Economics. The library was breathtaking. It appeared to have every book in the world on every conceivable theme. This place became Carmen's personal paradise. But she also had a personal sadness inside and an unresolved issue.

The issue between Carmen and Amanda

No! said Amanda. It could never be that way between us!

Amanda pulled away from Carmen's embrace. The girls had spent the afternoon in the park and walked to Carmen's house together. Amanda had a tough day and had been telling Carmen about it.

Carmen was very sympathetic. There was a moment when Amanda put her head on Carmen's shoulder. Carmen had held her softly. Their lives touched. Carmen wanted to tell Amanda how she felt about her. She wanted to express the special affection she had for her. They were lifelong friends. Carmen had struggled with this dilemma for about a year now, but she never said anything. Maybe now was the time. Amanda was shocked. Although she loved Carmen as a friend, an intimate relationship between the two girls was impossible.

"This can go no further! You can't tell anyone about this. We will keep this a secret between the two of us." Amanda implored.

Carmen agreed sadly. It wasn't her fault that she felt this way. She loved Amanda in a way that Amanda could not accept. Amanda didn't feel the same way about her. She accepted that with great melancholy.

Amanda held Carmen's hand and assured her that they would always be friends. This would not come between them. They kept the secret forever, but a shadow was cast.

The Cortez. Family Tragedy

Fernando beamed with pride as he drove Myra in the new Chevrolet. The Cortez family was the only family in the neighborhood who could afford a new car. A few other families had cars, but their cars were usually bought second hand for about one hundred dollars. Fernando drove his four-thousand-dollar car with pride. They stopped off at the Bodega to show the auto to the Ramos.

After a few cervezas (beers), Fernando and Myra got back into the car and drove onto the Brooklyn-Queens expressway. The kids were in school, and they had a few hours to themselves. Fernando had the day off. Fernando entered the highway on Atlantic Avenue. In his enthusiasm, he stepped on the gas harder. The beers were clouding his judgment. He laughed. Myra laughed. They gazed at each other. Fernando kept his foot on the pedal. He didn't see the truck that had stopped in their lane. There was an accident.

A police officer showed up at Carmen's school. He looked grim. He appeared to have trouble speaking. He didn't know where to begin. The school secretary ushered him into the principal's office. A few moments later, the principal came out of her office looking dismayed and horrified.

The policeman came out of the principal's office. He and the principal went to get the Cortez children out of their classes. Carmen and Fernando Jr. sat quietly in the back of the patrol car—not even looking at each other. Both knew something was terribly wrong. When they reached Bergen Street, Emilia Ramos was standing in front of their house. She had already identified the bodies of their parents.

She had wanted to save the children from that agonizing task. The car stopped and Emilia ran over to them. She held them tightly in her arms. She was their mother now.

Carmen's world turned black. She hurt too bad to cry. She didn't feel or hear anything around her. Mrs. Ramos' kind attempts to comfort her and her friends' constant companionship didn't alleviate her pain. The Ramos family took Carmen and her brother to their home above the bodega. Carmen sat by the front window wrapped in an old blanket for several days—not bothering to change her clothes or wash up. Elaine, Maria, and Amanda came to see her every day. They didn't know what to say. The priest from St. Agatha's church said at the funeral mass that Fernando and Myra Cortez were fortunate because they no longer had to feel the pain of this earth. They didn't but she, Carmen, surely did.

It was almost the end of the school year. Carmen did not go back to school. She passed her class grades even though she didn't go in to take the final exams. Her parents' house, which Fernando had willed to her and her brother, was boarded up. Carmen and Fernando stayed with Emilia Ramos. Fernando Jr. worked in the store that summer. Carmen helped too but mostly inside the house. Carmen began to learn how to cope with a wound that she knew would never heal. The months went by slowly. Carmen buried herself in her books in the private school for which her father had left the money.

Carmen and Fernando's aunt shows up.

"They will go with me!" shrieked the woman. "They will not!" replied Emilia Ramos angrily.

Carmen had never seen Mrs. Ramos so livid. She was screaming so loud that she was turning red. Perspiration poured down her forehead covering her face in its entirety.

"I am the natural aunt!" thundered the stranger.

"Really, how nice. Where were you when their parents died?" returned, Emilia.

"I didn't know. Nobody communicated with us in Puerto Rico. said the aunt.

A crowd of neighbors gathered outside the store as Carmen and Fernando came home from school. They now walked home from the school in Brooklyn Heights.

"Myra never gave me the names or addresses of Fernando's family in Puerto Rico. Myra's family all work on a farm and are poor. They can't take care of the kids. Those children are now my responsibility." reasoned Emilia.

"I am Fernando's sister. Their paternal aunt." said the woman, calming.

"Fernando didn't keep in touch with us because my parents opposed his marriage to Myra. If you knew him, you' d know that." informed the woman.

The stranger was Fernando's only sister, Mercedes Cortez. She had heard about her brother's tragic death through one of Myra's brothers in Puerto Rico. He gave her the name and address of the Ramos' family. Mercedes traveled to Puerto Rico frequently to visit her parents, but she had been living in Boston, Massachusetts for the last ten years. She came to get the niece and nephew she had never met. She was determined to give them a home. Mercedes had studied Business Administration in the University of Puerto Rico and came to Boston University to get an M.B.A. She was offered a job within the university and stayed there. She was a forty-year-old woman who had never married and had no children of her own.

Mercedes had taken the precaution of getting a lawyer and had filed papers for legal custody. Emilia Ramos had gone to school up to the eighth grade and had no knowledge of the court system. It had never occurred to her or her husband to file legal papers to keep the Cortez kids. Their mother had been her dear friend and she felt it was the least she could do. Besides, she had surely come to love them as her own. She's gladly give her own life for them. But the law was not on her side.

Mercedes went to her car and called her lawyer on her car phone. The man drove up to the bodega in a BMW and presented copies of the legal papers giving Mercedes custody. The signatures of Myra's parents were there. They felt that since she and her family had money, Carmen and Fernando Jr. would be better off with her.

Carmen couldn't believe what she was hearing. Standing before her was an outsider dressed in expensive designer clothes telling the hard working, Christian, store owner that she had come to take her and her brother to Boston. Carmen's world fell apart again. She didn't know what to say. She didn't know what to think. How many disruptions would there be in her life?

Emilia could not stop the tears which involuntarily flowed down her cheeks. The valiant facade broke down. Her heart dissolved as she realized that she was defeated. Carmen held her tight knowing that this would be the last hug. This was probably the last time she'd see this extraordinary woman who had become her mother.

Mercedes yelled impatiently "Carmen, get away from that dirty bodegera!"

"The chauffeur is waiting. Get in the car."

Emilia woke from her daze. She ran into the store and grabbed the butcher knife that she used to cut the meats and ran towards Mercedes. Several neighbors interceded while Mercedes ran into her car. The lawyer called the police on his car phone. The knife fell to the floor. One of the neighborhood children who had been watching the melee kicked the knife under a parked car. The child's mother, a neighborhood woman, stood near the car so that the police wouldn't think to look there when they arrived. Within minutes the police sirens could be heard.

By this time, Angelica Abate was standing with Emilia Ramos holding her hand to console her. The tall policeman exited the car and walked to the bodega where several women and children were standing. The Puerto Ricans tried to look natural. The lawyer ran up to the officer and said that Mrs. Ramos had threatened his client with a knife. At this point, Mrs. Abate said that Mrs. Ramos was a very good Christian. Her husband was the pastor of the Pentecost Church in this community and that there was no knife. The knife was safely nestled under the car, but the lawyer hadn't seen where the child had kicked it. The officer could not find the knife, and no one would verify the lawyer's story. The officer left.

Emilia called the woman who helped hide the knife into the store. Her name was Lydia. Emilia told her to take whatever groceries she needed. Lydia said she didn't have money. Emilia knew that.

"Take what you need. I know that by this time of the month you are probably short on food." said Emilia sweetly.

"But I owe you so much money." replied Lydia.

"You owe me nothing. I am canceling your past debt." The groceries you take today are free also." said Emilia solidly.

"How can I ever repay you? asked Lydia.

"How can I ever repay you? You kept me out of jail today." said Emilia.

"Que Dios la bendiga." responded Lydia.

"Que Dios la bendiga." said Emilia.

Emilia felt that it was the dawn of her life. The sun shone on the brownstones reflecting its rays on the otherwise shoddy street. Javier rode home on his truck tired and hungry. The moment he saw his wife, he knew there was something wrong. He put his arms around her and she crumpled in his grasp. Emilia had held back her tears until now. In the arms of her husband, her tears flowed. She sobbed wildly because her heart was breaking. She felt safe in her husband's embrace.

The girls graduate high school and go to college.

Stop daydreaming! said Maria.

I'm not daydreaming. said Elaine.

The girls were studying for final exams and Maria was having a hard time getting Elaine to concentrate. Elaine tried and tried, but it was so hard. These were the final exams they needed to graduate. Maria had already been accepted to New York University. Elaine hadn't gotten any positive responses yet. Amanda had gotten accepted to Barnard College, Columbia University. They even offered her a full scholarship. Maria got a generous offer from New York University. Carmen had written that she would be attending Boston University. She didn't have to pay tuition because her aunt worked for the university. She was going to attend the School of Management and major in Business Administration.

Gowanus Park had always been a place of solace. It's where the girls always went to discuss their good times and afflictions. But today Elaine sat alone. She hadn't bothered to call any of her friends. On her lap, she held the letters of rejection.

Dear Ms. Rivera,

"Thank you for your interest in our university. After careful consideration of your application, we regret to inform you that you were not accepted at this time."

She had five such letters. Her older siblings had all gone to college. Her three best friends had all gotten accepted to the colleges of their choice. SHE WAS REJECTED. She held out hope that she would be accepted to one of the Community Colleges, but they hadn't answered yet. She felt DUMB. Throughout her years, she had always worked hard at school. She was very rarely absent. It wasn't that she was lazy or that she was a delinquent. She came from a Christian family, and she didn't drink or do drugs.

Why had God sent her this challenge? A learning disability was something one couldn't see or hear. It was just something that happened. Maria said that she was smart in other ways. But Maria never told her in what ways she was smart. The Rivera family had made many sacrifices so that she, Elaine, could go to Catholic school—St. Agatha's, and then the high school. Now, she couldn't even get into a decent college. Was it all a waste of time and money? Her mother had said that the Catholic schools had given her a good education in a warm and pleasant environment. That was true but was that enough? Elaine knew that the school was not responsible for all the rejections. Elaine was despondent. Her future seemed so uncertain, and the outlook looked bleak.

Life on Bergen Street carried on despite the adversities faced by its residents. A person could look out of the window and see a show free of charge. It was not one of those streets that was ever desolate.

The artery was always saturated. People set up tables and played cards and dominoes. People played guitars and sang songs—some of which they made up themselves. Mothers sat on stoops and watched their children play. Babies reclined peacefully in strollers while their mothers gossiped about the neighbors.

Elaine walked around just wondering. She felt like a failure. Her dreams of becoming a registered nurse were shattered. Her three best friends would go on with their lives, but she would remain immobile. Although Maria and Amanda were so good to her, she missed Carmen miserably. Carmen had been the very first friend she had ever had. Now she perceived herself to be so alone. Her parents had taught her to have faith in God. She tried desperately to have faith now.

The graduation parties

Maria, Amanda, and Elaine decided that they wanted to celebrate their graduations together. Dona Angelica volunteered her substantial frame apartment. The other families agreed. Dona Emilia Ramos donated lots of food and beverages (soft drinks and coffee). The Ramos family were Pentecost and would not consume alcoholic beverages, and they surely wouldn't donate them for a party. Dona Angelica made new curtains and slip covers for the timeworn parlor furniture. Dona Lourdes, Amanda's Mom, brought a record player. The girls pooled their collection of records. The Abate, Martinez, Rivera, and Ramos families partied all night. A friendship that started on the first day of first grade at St. Agatha's had endured twelve years and was becoming more powerful each day.

The girls would face new challenges in college and their families would grow with them. But on this comely night, there was no anxiety and there were no quandaries. Life was glorious.

Bergen Street had started to change also—just as the girls were changing. Many owners were renovating their buildings. The entire neighborhood was becoming gentrified. Rents were skyrocketing and many residents had to move if they weren't covered by the rent control or rent stabilization laws. Elaine's family lived in the projects, so they didn't worry about the rising price of rent. Maria and Amanda's families were in rent-controlled apartments and could not be evicted. So, they stayed and watched the community change.

Javier and Emilia Ramos sold their store and the building above it, which they also owned, for a large amount of money and retired to Puerto Rico. The new owners renovated the building and turned the bodega into the base for a Car and Limousine Service. Several families sold their dwellings for large sums and either went back home or moved to Long Island or Westchester County. Carmen's aunt sold the Cortez home and placed the money in a trust fund for Carmen and Fernando Jr. Carmen did not come into town for the closing.

Chapter Four

College

Amanda and her mom rode the number 1 train from Times Square to the Columbia University Campus. It was the day of orientation and the new freshmen had been invited to stay for three nights to see the university and different aspects of it. Everything was free for Amanda. Although she had gone to her neighborhood high school with all the troublemakers, she was accepted to an Ivy League university and given a full scholarship. Lourdes was so proud. She never said so to Amanda, but she greatly admired how her daughter had been able to deal with adversity in the family at such a young age. She would tell her one day. She just needed to find the right words. Her paradox was how to tell Amanda that she, her daughter, had been her source of strength during her husband's illness. Lourdes loved her daughter because she was her daughter. She liked her daughter because of all the good qualities Amanda had demonstrated. She respected her daughter because of her profundity and kindness to family members and friends.

The train rambled on. The ride appeared endless. Finally, they reached the 116th station in Manhattan. As they exited the train station, they saw hundreds of students and parents also carrying overnight bags. Lourdes' heart sang. This was truly a dream come true. All the years of working in a factory had paid off. Amanda would get an excellent education and be somebody.

SOMEBODY BIG. SOMEBODY WHO WOULD BE RESPECTED IN THIS WORLD. Sadly, she remembered that she had been unable to pay a Catholic school when the other girls' parents could. Lourdes thought she would faint. There was a building with a huge sign saying WELCOME FRESHMEN and they went in there. Amanda took out her invitation to the event and was given her room number and keys. The orientation was three days long.

Lourdes and Amanda went to the assigned building and took the elevator to the sixth floor. The room was clean and large. There were no decorations of any sort. It was a single room. Lourdes opened the window to let the air in. The sun shone brightly inside, adorning the room with its golden rings. A young, Hispanic girl appeared at the door and introduced herself as" Evelyn". She said that she was the team leader for Amanda's group and would be guiding her through the scheduled activities. She invited her to come and meet some of the other girls. There were about a dozen Hispanic girls assembled in Evelyn's room. All of them were dressed comfortably and all appeared enthusiastic about the upcoming events.

Lourdes gave Amanda some money and left with bittersweet feelings. She had hoped to stay a little longer and roam the campus for a while with her daughter. Instead, Amanda had been swept away by other collegians. She ambled slowly down the hallways and into the elevator. She tucked her hard, sore hands into her pockets. She didn't want to expose the work worn hands of a dressmaker in this prestigious university. The number 1 train traveled along towards Times Square. Lourdes felt very, very lonely. She realized that this was the first time that Amanda had spent a night away from home.

Meanwhile, Miranda sat at her kitchen table; the same one that they brought from Puerto Rico years ago. Her heart ached as she thought about her youngest child, Elaine, and wondered how to help her. Miranda had gone to school up to the eighth grade in Puerto Rico. The older children were all married and had families of their own. They had had no difficulties in school. Elaine's behavior in school had always been excellent. She never did drugs or ran around with the wrong crowd.

She always tried to learn. She never missed any days of school except when she was sick. In four years of high school, she was absent three days because of flu in third year. Still, she couldn't get into college. Miranda wanted Elaine to get a good education and be able to take care of herself. The parents would not last forever.

Meanwhile, Maria Abate beamed with pride as she and her mother rode the train into the West Village to New York University. Maria knew that the Education program was excellent, and she'd be a great teacher when she graduated. The Village seemed like such an interesting place. Maria had heard of it but had never really walked through it. There were young people with colors in their hair and rings on their nostrils. WOW!

This was another world. Maria had never genuinely been outside of her neighborhood. South Brooklyn seemed so far away. She was here for an orientation to which parents had also been invited.

Maria reached the front door of The Washington Square College of Arts and Sciences. She turned to talk to Angelica when she bumped her right shoulder into a young man who was also looking for the freshman orientation.

"Excuse me'." said Maria.

"It's okay." said Orlando Rodriguez. "I'm not going to die."

"Okay." said Maria with a big smile.

They went their separate ways to look for the orientation desk. Maria and Angelica reached the desk just about the same time that Orlando and his mother did. They both smiled again. Maria thought that he was probably the most handsome guy she had ever seen. But she had to focus on what she was doing there that day. She told herself that she wasn't in college to look for boys but to study and make her mother proud. Angelica had told Maria that she should not complain about the problems in their community, but that she should get an education and come back and help her own people. Maria intended to do just that. She thought sadly of her father who would have been so proud. She hoped that he was looking down on her from heaven.

He'd be so proud of her. Estefano had only been in school up to the fourth grade in Europe. Maria shifted her line of thought to her registration. The girl behind the table took the cards and gave her a pile of papers. She sat down at some old desks which had been placed for the convenience of incoming freshmen and began to fill them out. She chose courses in Education, Spanish, Biology, and English literature. Maria had just taken her first step towards becoming a teacher. This was the first step towards her dream. Classes started in just two days. Dona Angelica was dazzled by all the papers.

When that formidable chore was completed, they walked over to the room where the orientation was located. There were cakes, cookies, pastries, coffee, and soft drinks. Everyone was so friendly. It was approaching noon, Maria and Angelica were famished. The fare presented was most gratifying. The president of the college welcomed the freshmen. Maria tried to understand everything he said while Angelica smiled warmly pretending, she understood. Maria thought she saw Orlando looking at her from across the room, but she tried not to look back.

While Maria and Amanda attended orientation, there were no fancy orientations for Elaine Rivera. There were no acceptances to big name universities or overtures of scholarships or grants. But Miranda had the heart of a tiger and wasn't going to let that stop her. Miranda did not know what a learning disability was, and she refused to believe her daughter was unintelligent. She would find a way to help her. She was going to get a better education somehow. Miranda just didn't know what she was going to do. This kitchen looked so dismal, and instantaneously Miranda was weary of this apartment, of this public housing project, and of this city.

Miranda swallowed her pride and called Elaine's former guidance counselor at her high school. It was early September, and the other girls were just now registering. She figured there was time for Elaine to start school somewhere. Miranda didn't want Elaine to take just any unskilled job. Besides, Miranda had never taken a civil service test, but she knew Elaine would have trouble passing any of them.

The guidance counselor was very attentive when Miranda called her. She told Miranda that she could come down that very day. Miranda thanked her and began to get ready. The only time that she had seen that high school was when Elaine graduated. Dona Angelica took both Elaine and Maria for registration.

As she rode the N train, Miranda thought about how rarely she left the projects and her neighborhood. Guillermo traveled the whole city driving his passengers around. There was no neighborhood that he was not familiar with. Miranda, however, rarely left her home. She shopped and did her banking in her community. She washed the family's clothes in the local laundromat. In the neighborhood all the people spoke Spanish, and she rarely had to use English. The older children had left home, but most of them didn't live too far away. They came to visit her; she rarely visited them. Since her arrival from Puerto Rico, her life had revolved around this neighborhood.

As Miranda reached the school, she wondered how Elaine had been able to hold her own in such an impressive looking lyceum. She felt a surge of pride. Miranda went to the front desk and proceeded to explain that she was there to see Miss Maresca. The security guard had already been notified to expect her. Miranda was given a pass and the counselor's room number. Miranda walked timidly up the stairs to the second floor. The girls looked so profound in their uniforms.

Miss Maresca met her at the door. She extended her hand and said that she was very happy to meet Elaine's mother at last. Miranda smiled brightly holding the counselor's hand. She felt comfortable as soon as she entered the office.

"I am sorry that I do not speak much English". Miranda apologized.

"I understand you perfectly. Besides, I speak a little Spanish." said Miss Maresca warmly.

"How can I help you?" asked Miss Maresca.

"I don't know where to begin." said Miranda, showing great affliction.

"I came to ask a favor." she continued.

"My Elaine did not get accepted into any of the colleges she applied to. She is very sad and disappointed with herself. I am worried about her future. I would like her to get some sort of skills with which to earn a living. I don't know where else to turn." disclosed Miranda.

"I am happy that you came to see me." said Miss Maresca in words she felt Miranda would understand.

"I think that I might be able to help if Elaine will let me. She never told me about all the rejections, although I suspected. She didn't give us a name of a college when we collected the information for the yearbook. I thought that she just didn't want to go to college. Elaine never consulted with me. I wish I had known. I would have been able to help her before." informed Miss Maresca.

"Is it too late?" inquired Miranda.

"No, it isn't. There are good schools that will accept Elaine." said the Counselor.

She took out several circulars. These were brochures from several vocational schools. Elaine had been interested in nursing. So, the guidance counselor showed the schools that gave courses in nursing. There was one school which trained young women to become L.P.N. s or licensed practical nurses. Miss Maresca explained that the title of R.N. was more impressive, but the L.P.N. also worked closely with patients and were very valuable in the hospitals. She was sure that Elaine would be accepted. The tuition could be covered by a student loan and Elaine could begin to pay it back six months after she graduated. The school also had job placement services. Miss Maresca called the school and made an appointment for Elaine and Miranda to go for an interview. Miranda thanked the counselor with enthusiasm. She was immensely grateful.

As Miranda rode the train back home, she couldn't believe that she had done something constructive that could help her daughter. She didn't have to ask her husband or one of her older children for help. She came up with an idea and worked on it. God had placed Miss Maresca there to help them. She thanked God and said a silent prayer for Miss Maresca. She was sure Elaine would be pleased. As she commuted on the subway, she felt joy, peace, and fulfillment. She was reconciled with the fact that Elaine wasn't going to be a doctor or a lawyer, but she was going to do something good in her life.

Several days later, Elaine approached the school, which was walking distance from her house, with cautious optimism. She had been hurt so many times by rejections that she didn't want to presume anything positive.

The interior of the school looked better than the outside. It was immaculate and businesslike. There were rows of basic chairs in the lobby. A receptionist greeted prospective students and their parents in a pleasant manner. After a few moments, a representative came out to greet them. The young man had already been advised that they were coming by Miss Maresca and had already received Elaine's academic transcript.

Mr. Sommers reviewed the transcript with Elaine and advised her that she would have to take a placement test. Once she was accepted, she would complete her program in about eighteen months if she passed all the courses. Elaine smiled slightly at the prospect of having a valid credential in less than two years. Elaine took the test, signed the papers for the student loans, and went home to wait for an answer.

Elaine gets accepted to vocational school.

The park welcomed Elaine with a gentle breeze. Just a few days ago, she paused there on the same seat tears flowing gently down her cheeks. Her life seemed cheerless. Today, she had some hope. Her mother had guided and encouraged her. Her mother, who had barely left the projects since she had come from Puerto Rico, had made a trip to her former high school to talk to an English-speaking guidance counselor. Most surprisingly, Miranda Rivera had connected and helped her daughter find a solution. There were alternative ways of getting an education. Elaine herself should have thought of that. But she had wanted to be like her friends. All three of them were going to prestigious four-year universities. Elaine decided that she would go to this school if she was accepted and do her best. She would find her happiness. Whatever she did in this life, she would be productive. She got accepted.

Miranda always told her children that people were like stars. Each one had its appointed place. Well, that was true, and she would find her appointed place. She felt the heartache of rivalry as she thought of the others in college. But she knew that she had to overcome those feelings. Her friends Carmen and Amanda had always helped her with her schoolwork in St. Agatha's. Maria helped her in high school. She might never have graduated without their help. Elaine walked over to St. Agatha's church. She sat in the back pew for a while and prayed for her success in her new school and the success of her friends in their new endeavors.

Meanwhile, Amanda ran feverishly from one class to another—Biology, Chemistry, Psychology, and ah, British Literature. She didn't like that last one, but she approached it with devotion anyway. There was just so much to learn! Amanda's mind engrossed in the wisdom thrown at her as if the world were coming to an end. She was finally where she wanted to be. This was the university she had always dreamed about. In her daydreams, she always imagined herself in an educational setting of this sort. She spent hours on end in the Columbia University library. The "stacks" were a great place to study. There was so much privacy. Columbia seemed to have bought every book in the world. Although Amanda didn't worry much about grades, she was doing very well. Because she loved to study, the marks flowed graciously with no apparent effort on her part.

At the same time, Maria sat at her kitchen table with the stew boiling softly as she read her textbook on education. The work was hard and so she studied intensely. She worked wholly and diligently. She had just come home from school and had started dinner. Dona Angelica had not yet come home from the garment center. By the time her mother came home, dinner would be ready. Maria paused a moment to start the salad. She had already cut up the vegetables for the stew.

There was a gentle knock on the front door. Maria knew it was not her mother so early. She looked through the peek hole and noticed Elaine standing outside.

"Wow, what a pleasant surprise!" said Maria, sincerely.

"Yeah, I haven't seen you for a while. "Just thought I'd come by and say hello." explained Elaine.

"I've been meaning to call. I'm taking all these hard courses." said Maria, remorsefully.

"It's all right. I understand. I wanted to show you my books and tell you about my courses." said Elaine.

"Great, I've got dinner on. Stay and we'll talk." said Maria, cheerfully.

Maria was really pleased to see Elaine. She thought about going to her house a thousand times but lacked the courage. Maria never figured t at Elaine would have so much trouble getting into college. She did not know what to say to her. She was so relieved that Elaine had taken the first step.

"Stay for dinner." continued Maria.

Maria went to the kitchen and came back with two cans of Pepsi. The girls sat on the big vintage sofa. The new slipcovers danced with delight anytime someone sat down.

"I've really missed you." said Maria. Elaine still hadn't said anything.

"I am working very hard. The courses are intense." commented Maria.

Elaine was Maria's best friend except for Amanda, but she felt awkward currently. She rambled on and on about insignificant things, trying desperately to break the ice. Finally, Elaine spoke.

"I am really happy for you." stated Elaine, in a sincere tone.

"Ever since the first grade, you, Carmen, and Amanda have always been smarter than me. It was not a surprise that you all got scholarships to big name colleges and I didn't. But I've thought about it, and I've come to realize that it doesn't matter. We were always friends anyway. I probably wouldn't have gotten through high school without your help. Besides I like the school that I am in now." Elaine affirmed.

Maria could barely contain her delight. She had not wanted to lose Elaine's friendship. She thought that Elaine might drift away from her. But now she knew they'd always be friends and her heart sang.

Elaine recounted how her mother had gone to the guidance counselor on her own and sought help. Maria remembered Miss Maresca fondly. She explained how the guidance counselor had gone through brochures from several different schools and made the appointment for the one that offered nursing. Elaine felt that the courses offered were appropriate for her. She understood the teachers and was able to do her schoolwork on her own. This was a source of pride for her.

Elaine stayed for dinner with Maria and Dona Angelica. They talked into the night. Maria told Elaine about Orlando who was on a sports scholarship. He was majoring in Physical Education, but he wanted to be a professional baseball player. Some of the other students didn't have a good opinion of the students on sports scholarships, but Maria felt that it was no one's business. The athletes helped the university make money by attracting viewers to the games. The revenue from these games was a valuable source of income for the colleges. But Maria didn't care about what Orlando was majoring in. She didn't care how he paid his tuition. He was kind and sweet and she was so flattered when he followed her around the campus.

Elaine had also met someone interesting. He was a young auto mechanic who was a friend of one of her brothers. She hadn't thought much of him being an auto mechanic, but he had a diploma from a professional trade school and was making good money. He hoped to have a shop of his own one day, but he was in line to inherit his father's shop. His name was Domingo. He had asked her out to dinner, but she had refrained. Elaine was shy and quiet by nature. She had never actually gone out of a date and wasn't sure how to react. Twelve years of Catholic school had taught her to be a good Christian and a good person but hadn't shown what to expect on a date. Dona Angelica smiled quietly during this conversation. The girls were grown up and would have families of their own in a few years. She was beginning to accept the idea.

Amanda's College Experiences

"Stop daydreaming. You're going to blow up the lab! bellowed Amanda. Another student had just mixed in the wrong chemicals in the chemistry lab. They now had to start over. Amanda couldn't understand why other students weren't as hardworking and dedicated as she was. The girls had to work in groups of two and Amanda did not particularly like her appointed partner. Amanda was determined to do well. She was dedicated and had problems dealing with someone else's mediocrity. She would save lives with the medical skills she intended to acquire.

After the lab, she went to her next class. She had the paper that was due today. She'd never dream of going to class unprepared. Amanda had never been particularly social and was not making a great effort to make friends on campus. She was there to study and learn. She had been given a scholarship which was contingent on her grades. After having attended one of the toughest and most dangerous high schools in New York, she wasn't going to lose her scholarship.

At home Lourdes often asked Amanda how school was going. She and Dona Angelica often compared notes about their respective daughters. Amanda seemed so engrossed in her studies. This was good of course; however, it was not good to forget about her old friends and her family. Amanda barely talked to her father anymore. She never appeared to have the time. There was never much to say. Lourdes loved the idea of Amanda obtaining a higher education but worried about her losing her tender qualities.

One Friday night, Amanda and her family were surprised by a sudden knock on the door. Amanda was absorbed in her books as usual. Lourdes answered the door and in burst Maria and Elaine followed by Dona Angelica. Maria carried a pile of records and Elaine carried a cake baked by her mother. Lourdes and Angelica exchanged winks. The girls ran into Amanda's room.

As the music flowed, the girls exchanged experiences. Maria was almost "dating" Orlando who was the son of a Pentecostal minister. She had her mother's blessing. He was Puerto Rican and had been born in Puerto Rico. He had lived on a farm. He had a younger sister.

Elaine told Amanda about her new school. She was taking courses in anatomy and physiology. Amanda thought to herself that these courses were probably modified for students like Elaine, but she didn't say anything. Elaine had gone on two double dates with Domingo. One of her older brothers and his wife had gone with them. Elaine would graduate in about a year. Amanda was pleased.

Domingo proposes marriage to Elaine.

"When are you going to tell them?" implored Domingo. "Not now. It's not the right time." answered Elaine firmly.

"Not until I get my diploma and find a job." continued Elaine.

"You can at least tell them that we want to get married. We are not going to get married tomorrow. Give them time to understand and accept our decision." said Domingo, trying desperately to convince Elaine.

"I'll try. But my mom thinks that if I fall in love, I won't finish my schooling. She's worried about me not finishing my course." explained Elaine.

"Please try. Do what you can. Explain to your mother that we are not getting married until after you do graduate." said Domingo relieved.

Domingo went back to his auto shop. He came to see Elaine everyday for lunch. He waited downstairs until she came out with the other students. Then they went to different fast-food restaurants in the area. This time of day was precious to both. What had started as a casual introduction had become a lifetime commitment for both.

Domingo looked forward to lunchtime every day. It was the only time that he and Elaine could speak privately. There were lots of girls out there who would marry him because his family owned an auto shop that he would inherit. Elaine was different.

She was sweet and innocent. She was hard working at home and in school. She was Catholic and had not been running around with other men. Elaine was the kind of young woman that a man brought home to meet his mother. She was the type of woman with whom a man settled down and had a family There were girls who men "ran around with" for a while and discarded when they tired of them. Elaine was special. Elaine was the future "Mrs. Perez". Domingo went to work happily knowing that he was building a future for Elaine and the family that they would have together.

Winter approached quickly. Bergen Street was capped with snowflakes and the community were starting to think of Christmas which is the most solemn of Christian holy days. For the people of Puerto Rico, the Christmas season doesn't end until after the sixth of January, the Day of the Three Kings.

With the coming of the holiday season, came the end of the first semester in college for the girls. All had a sense of triumph. This recess provided a chance to get together. The park was delightful with its new ivory covering. Amanda, Maria, and Elaine cleared a bench and huddled to exchange ideas. The mighty oak trees inclined to listen to the girls' adventures. They wouldn't tell the girl's parents. Amanda thought about how wonderful it was to see Elaine smile again. She appeared to be truly happy.

"Sorry, I was daydreaming". apologized Maria.

The other girls looked at her with merriment in their eyes. Then they glanced at each other. Maria had not been following their conversation. Sitting on an antiquated bench in the park with her two best friends, Maria was daydreaming and chuckling to herself.

"Why don't you just tell us what you're thinking about? "I am dying of curiosity." inquired Amanda with genuine interest.

Elaine listened quietly. She sensed what Maria was going to say, but she listened politely. She didn't want to interrupt and spoil Maria's explanation. Maria began to speak slowly.

She told Elaine and Amanda that she and Orlando had not known each other very long but he appeared to be becoming serious. She had told her mother about him. Although she wasn't as interested in him as he was in her at this time, she knew she wanted to get to know him better. She'd love to invite him home to dinner. But she was afraid at how her mother would feel about a relationship currently. Maria had never actually been on a date. Besides, she had to keep up her grades to keep her scholarship. She didn't want to become distracted and flunk out of school.

Maria spoke on but she knew, and her friends knew, that she was simply airing out her own insecurities. She was a Catholic school girl who was entering young womanhood and she wasn't sure how to handle her feelings and emotions especially with respect to this young man.

"You want to hear what I think?" inquired Amanda.

"I think he sounds fine, but you are right about not getting too serious too fast." volunteered Amanda, without Maria's approval.

"There's plenty of time for that." added Elaine, favorably.

Elaine had her own experience to convey. She told the girls about Domingo who worked in his father's auto repair shop. Domingo, being an only child, would inherit everything. That's not why Elaine liked him. She felt that he was kind, sweet, and honest. He was so hardworking, a quality she valued. Amanda raised her eyes at Elaine's enthusiasm for an auto-mechanic, but she kept her feelings to herself. Years later, she'd regret that negative thought.

Amanda told the girls about her studies and the courses she was taking. They all sounded so hard. Amanda had met lots of the other students at Columbia, but she really hadn't formed any attachments. She studied almost all the time. Amanda dreamed of being a doctor and marrying a doctor. She would save lives. She would work in an inner-city hospital where she would treat children just like herself. In all her own daydreams, she never thought of putting up an office on Park Avenue for rich people. That was not for her.

At home, later that night, Amanda deliberated how the others were forming relationships with men and she was not. She thought about that experience with Carmen years ago. An encounter that she had never shared with anyone, not even her mother. Amanda did not understand what Carmen was trying to say to her. She marveled at how Carmen could have crystallized that kind of amour for her, a childhood friend. It really didn't matter much now. Carmen's parents died shortly afterwards, and Carmen was at Boston University. She hoped to see Carmen again one day and perhaps discuss this issue in a mature way. Carmen wrote letters to the other two girls but not to her. Amanda only received Christmas cards with generic holiday greetings. This caused her some pain, but she couldn't consent to Carmen's invocation. She still wanted Carmen's friendship, but she sensed she had lost that.

If Gowanus Park could talk, it would have told all the girls 'triumphs during the year 1972—1973. May brought forth the completion of the first year of higher education. The mighty oak trees welcomed the girls to their reserved seat on the antiquated bench.

Amanda was going to take summer classes covered by her scholarship. Elaine was doing her internship at a local hospital which had been arranged by her school. Maria was going to be a teacher's assistant in the Gowanus Day Care Center. The year appeared to have flown by.

Elaine Gets Married

Mr. and Mrs. Guillermo Rivera request the pleasure of
your company at the wedding of their daughter.
Elaine to
Mr. Domingo Perez
April 15, 1974
St. Patrick s Cathedral
1 p.m.
Reception at The Camille Manor

The neighborhood could not have been more surprised. Amanda and Maria were dazzled. The girls had forgotten that Elaine's course was only eighteen months long and she said that she would marry when she graduated. They hadn't spoken lately. Carmen was coming to be the maid of honor. Amanda, Maria, and Elaine's sister were all going to be Bride's maids. Elaine would be almost twenty years old on the day of her wedding. Domingo was twenty-two. The wedding was going to be held in St. Patrick's Cathedral because Elaine had always dreamed to marrying in St. Patrick's. The reception would be held in Brooklyn. Domingo was paying for everything because Elaine had informed him that her family could not pay for a wedding at this time. She said that she would work for a while and then get married. Domingo could not accept that. His family was rich compared to Elaine's. So, the wedding was scheduled.

"I don't believe it". said Maria truthfully. "I don't either." agreed Amanda.

"It's just so soon. She's so young and she's never dated any other guys. She's going from her parents' home to her husband's home." continued Maria.

"She's going from her parents' home to her own home." corrected Amanda.

"But can she handle that?" wondered Maria.

"It's not our business. Let's not say any of this to Elaine." said Amanda.

Dona Angelica volunteered to make Elaine's wedding dress and those of the bride's maids. That would be her wedding gift to Elaine. Dona Angelica did not have much money and she brought the material from her factory. She felt that she couldn't buy an appropriate gift, so she did what she could. Luckily, she had a month to work on the dresses. The Rivera family, especially Miranda and Elaine, were very grateful.

Carmen came into town the day before the wedding just in time for a final rehearsal. Her aunt, Mercedes, and her brother, Fernando, came also. She stayed at the Hilton in Manhattan which was not far from St. Patrick's Cathedral. Mercedes would not stay with any of the friends' families.

Carmen was at Boston University and studying commerce. She had just completed her second year. The School of Management was an acclaimed school of business. Carmen loved her courses and Boston was beautiful. But the girls sensed an emptiness within their friend. She looked cold and distant to a degree.

Despite how she appeared to the other girls, Carmen was very happy for her best friend, Elaine. She had always loved her like a sister and was delighted to be her maid of honor. She thought the dress that Dona Angelica had so lovingly sewn was splendid. Carmen didn't ask about Mrs. Ramos and didn't even mention her. The other girls pretended not to notice.

After the wedding, Carmen left quietly with just a quick hug to her friends. When she entered the limo, her aunt had hired to take the family to the airport, she didn't look back. Amanda and Maria went back to their classes. They had final exams coming up. Elaine went to work at Long Island College Hospital in their Brooklyn neighborhood after a two week honeymoon in El Dorado, Puerto Rico. She and Domingo moved into the second floor of his parents' two-family house. The house was one block away from his auto shop. Elaine was no longer a child. She was now a licensed practical nurse and a wife. She had a husband, a house, and a full-time job.

The Spring turned to Summer and the Summer turned to Fall and the Fall turned to Winter repeatedly. Although Washington Square Park was not Gowanus by any means, Maria studied on the benches there and dreamed of life when she graduated. It was the Fall of 1975 and if she passed her final exams she'd graduate at the end of May. She'd been happy here in Manhattan and she almost hated to leave this curious neighborhood. Maria had already made the arrangements to take the city test for bilingual teachers. She had taken the National Teaching Exam and got a good score. She felt confident in her ability to teach. It was something she was looking forward to. She sat in the park day after day studying and dreaming about her future reality. Orlando Rodriguez had come to play a major part in her existence. She and Orlando were having dinner with

Dona Angelica right after her major exams the next week. They intended to tell her about their wedding plans. The wedding date had been set by them for August 16, 1976. Maria shuddered at the thought of telling her mother. She knew Dona Angelica wanted her to get married but perhaps not so soon after graduation. Orlando and she felt that they had waited long enough to start their life together. He was also taking the teaching exam for Physical Education teachers. He had a job in a department store until he got appointed by the Board of Education. They had made their arrangement. They wanted a discreet wedding Mass in St. Agatha's church and a small reception at home. Orlando was content to marry in the Catholic church although his family was Pentecostal. What more could she ask for?

Amanda's challenge to get into medical school

"What? A rejection? Again?" yelled Amanda as she flung herself into her bed.

Amanda had applied to several medical schools and had so far received two rebuffs. This was too much for a young woman who was not used to being refused.

When Lourdes heard the cry, she came running from the kitchen. She scooped up Amanda in her arms and cradled her as she had when she was a baby. The mother didn't know what else she could do.

"Medical school is the hardest school in the world to get into". said the- mother sadly.

"Surely one of them will accept you." added Lourdes confidently.

"I hope so. My dream is to be a doctor. I will be a doctor." stated Amanda, trying to sound convinced.

She fell asleep in her mother's arms. The bittersweet darkness of night covered Bergen Street. as Lourdes implored the Almighty to remedy her daughter's pain. All things are possible in God repeated the faithful mother until sleep overcame her too.

Amanda's graduation was coming up in a couple of weeks and that would be something to look forward to. Tomorrow is another day. Things will look better tomorrow. At least, that's what this heartbroken mother hoped for anyway.

May is the most beautiful month of the year. There were no flowers to blossom on Bergen Street, but the leaves on the trees were green and the park was cleaned and ready for the neighborhood children. The Gowanus Park was always welcoming. Amanda and Maria sat in their usual place and talked. Maria wished that she could do something to help her friend. She had always known of Amanda's keen desire to be a doctor. Amanda had certainly worked very hard. She had gotten an almost perfect average. Maria had never seen anyone so dedicated.

"Most people who apply to medical schools get some rejections."

"I'm sure that you'll get an acceptance soon." said Maria.

"I hope you're right. Otherwise, I'll have worked so much for nothing." responded Amanda.

"Even if you don't get into medical school this year, you have an impressive degree from one of the best universities. There are so many things you can do.

You can get a great job in a hospital and reapply next year." consoled Maria.

"Yeah, right. Then I'll watch the real doctors at work and choke my own envy." said Amanda, without even trying to hide her antipathy.

"Let's walk over to Elaine's and see her baby. I'm sure she'll be happy to see us. Domingo's not home from work yet. We can talk and hang out." suggested Maria.

"Okay. I guess it's better than just sitting here on this bench complaining." answered Amanda.

Elaine had a lovely baby girl. She looked just like Elaine, and she was so sweet. Elaine had named the baby Carmen. She had taken a maternity leave to take care of her child. The baby was just about six or seven months old.

When Amanda and Maria arrived, Elaine was just starting dinner for her family. Her kitchen was immaculate, and she seemed to have all aspects of housekeeping under control. She was delighted to see the girls.

"Wow, what a pleasant surprise!" she said with genuine delight.

You're invited to take part in one of my luscious dinners. Arroz con glandules is on the menu. If you leave a big tip, I'll throw in a pastel." Added Elaine with a huge smile.

"I don't think that I can resist that." said Maria honestly.

Maria wondered how Elaine could do so much. She was their same age but here she was raising a family and running a household. She also had a professional diploma.

The girls helped Elaine set the table. Little Carmen woke up and Amanda rushed to pick her up out of the bassinet. The baby felt so soft and cuddly in her arms.

"One day I'll have a little angel like this one." said Amanda.

"So, will I. I'll have lots of them." added Maria.

"You and Orlando better get started then. said Amanda.

"When is the big day? I presume I'm invited." inquired Elaine.

"August 16th. I'll send out the invitations after I explain it all to my mom." answered Maria visibly shaken.

Domingo came home and they all had a pleasant dinner. Amanda felt so good, she almost forgot about the medical schools she had gotten rejected from. She quietly prayed for inner strength to deal with whatever came next.

Maria gets married.

"What? What are you talking about?" screamed Dona Angelica.

"Mom, I' m getting married. It's settled. I've decided." said Maria.

"You decided. Who gave you the authority to make decisions?" inquired Dona Angelica honestly.

"I'm twenty-two. I make my own decisions now." said Maria sadly but firmly.

"Really? Is that so? Just like that?" asked the poignant mother.

"Yes, Mom, just like that." answered her daughter resolutely.

"Who is going to pay for this wedding? Do you have money for a home of your own?" asked Angelica.

"We are going to pay for the wedding. The church costs $200.00, and we paid it already. We talked to a caterer who's charging $165.00 for the food. We'll set it up buffet style. Orlando's mother is buying the wedding cake and other pastries. We can have the reception in our apartment or his family's apartment. The invitations won't cost much to print out. We found an apartment in Queens and Orlando already has a job." answered Maria with amazing logic.

"You have everything figured out. You didn't consult me about anything. My opinion and my feelings were not important. Good luck." said Dona Angelica defeated at last.

The wedding was a quiet concern. Dona Angelica reluctantly accepted that her only daughter was marrying and starting a life of her own. Despite the limited funds available for the reception, the party turned out very good.

Amanda gets into medical school.

"MOM, THE WHOLE WORLD IS MINE". God has answered my prayer." roared Amanda.

Lourdes and Miguel Martinez came running when they heard the screams. There were papers all over the bedroom floor. Amanda had thrown them there. She held the letter in her hand. HER ACCEPTANCE!

After oodles of tears and a host of heartaches, she was going to medical school. HER DREAM HAD COME TRUE! The family read the letters carefully. Amanda had been accepted by Columbia University Medical School. She received some scholarship funds. She would take out a loan for the rest of it. Guillermo said he would pay the loans. He would work day and night if he had to, but he wasn't going to let his little girl down again. Not ever again!

Amanda wished that Columbia had written to her sooner, and that she wouldn't have had to suffer so much, but she was thankful anyway. She thanked God for His blessing to her. She would have called Maria, but she was away with Orlando on their honeymoon. So, she called Dona Angelica who was delighted to hear the news. She called Elaine who was also filled with joy. Amanda's torment lifted from her, and she had a new cause for living.

Maria goes to graduate school.

The New York City Board of Education was a big bureaucracy. Maria was frightened and Orlando was frustrated. However, they were both determined to take the tests and get their teaching licenses. They filled out the forms and submitted them to the clerk. They would have to wait to be called to come in and take the exams.

Orlando was working as an assistant manager of the Sports equipment section in a big department store in Manhattan. Maria had a full scholarship to Teachers' College to get her master's degree in Bilingual Special Education. Maria felt that not being able to work now was a good thing because she could dedicate her time to her new husband, her new home and getting her Masters' degree. However, there was someone else who would require Maria's attention—the new baby. Maria was surprised to be expecting so quickly.

Orlando was more surprised, but they owned up to their responsibility. Dona Angelica, who had recently retired from the garment district, moved into Maria's building in Queens to help with the baby. When she was born, they named her Angelica "Angie" for short.

Baby Angie was a handful. She was born a preemie and had plenty of compensating to do. She weighed five pounds which was a good weight for a baby born prematurely. Maria felt that it was very fortunate that her mother was able to come and help her. Angie was born towards the end of her first year of marriage. She finished her master's degree a few months later.

Maria becomes a Special Education Teacher.

Then it was time to go out and find a job. Dona Angelica joyfully volunteered to take care of her granddaughter who was now eighteen months old. The Board of Education offered Maria a job in the South Bronx. Maria was awed when she arrived at the school to which she had been assigned.

The Community Elementary school was an elementary school that housed grades kindergarten to fifth. It was in the South Bronx of New York City. The neighborhood was much poorer than the neighborhood Maria had grown up in Brooklyn. Many of the children came to school by bus.

The population was mostly African American and Hispanic. Maria was very curious about this new community to which she was being sent by the Board of Education. She and Orlando took the time to walk around and ask questions of store owners and residents. Orlando was worried about her safety and wellbeing. He was still going to be working in Manhattan and she'd be coming to work alone if she accepted the job. There were yet no positions for gym teachers and he'd have to wait until the Board called him.

Maria learned that the drug dealers had taken over many of the buildings and streets, and the police considered this one of the most dangerous war zones in the city. A branch of the Bronx Lebanon Hospital was right in front of the school. The ambulances could be seen from the school windows transporting patients.

The community was a very lively and interesting one. It was ethnically diverse. Although it was basically Hispanic and African American, the people were from were from different countries. There are a few families from Puerto Rico, some from Honduras, and some from Mexico. The largest group among the Hispanics was that from the Dominican Republic. There are African American families in which the parents were born here in the United States but there are many families from the West Indian Islands of Jamaica, Trinidad, and St. Thomas.

The neighborhood was made up mostly of large buildings-multi-family dwellings. Maria learned that many families complained of bad living conditions such as lack of heat and hot water, broken doors, and faulty windowpanes which allow drafts in the winter. That may not have been the case with every building but there have been numerous complaints.

There were single mothers in the neighborhood who were receiving public assistance benefits. The parents who were working for the most part did not receive high salaries. Many families did not have medical insurance if they did not qualify for Medicaid.

The environment was a lively one. The school was up the hill from Third Avenue. Third Avenue was a very busy street on which two buses ran. The avenue was always filled with people due to the bus stops and the stores. Third Avenue was basically lined with stores. On one corner was an Arab delicatessen. Next to it was a New Way supermarket in which all the employees were Hispanic. There was a huge public housing project which expanded several blocks. On the block perpendicular to the school was a Dominican restaurant, a Chinese restaurant, a bodega, and a coffee shop.

The physical structure of the school was pleasant. It was a cozy, pre-war building. There were four floors. Visitors entered through a front door at which the security guard stood and asked visitors to sign in. The front staircase was made of marble. It divided as it led to the second floor to where the general office was located. The general office also housed the principal's office.

The principal's office was spacious. Three secretaries worked in a common space-the pupil accounting secretary, the payroll secretary, and one who is really a school aide but worked in the office. The general office also housed the principal's office. The atmosphere was congenial. Maria did not observe any rudeness on the part of the office workers to parents or staff members.

The auditorium was right across from the general office. There were three doors to the auditorium. The side doors usually remained locked. The middle door was usually open. The auditorium was for assembly pro- grams and for taking care of children whose parents are late picking them up or whose bus came late.

There are classrooms to the right and left of the auditorium. The third floor housed the Teachers' room which was about the size of two classrooms combined. It had a refrigerator and a soda machine. There used to be a microwave and a television, but they were both stolen about three years before. They were never replaced.

In front of the Teachers' lounge was a computer lab. All the children had a period at the computer each day. Every child in the school was learning to use the computer from kindergarten to the fifth grade. The Special Education classes also used computer facilities. The computer lab was equipped to service two classes at one time.

Maria liked the way the classes were structured. There were two bilingual first grade classes and three monolingual first grade classes on the second floor. This was the first floor that was used for instruction. The first floor housed the hot lunchroom and the cold lunchroom. There was also a special class called a cycle class which runs for six weeks and taught children who were in regular first grade but had some academic problems. Every six weeks the monolingual teachers submitted three names of children who required special help with Reading and Mathematics. These children were then placed in this cycle class. They were taught by two teachers in a smaller group than in their regular class. The Guidance Counselor's office was also on the second floor.

The third floor of the school housed classrooms for the second-grade bilingual and monolingual as well as a bilingual third grade class and one monolingual third grade class. The assistant principal for the upper grades also had an office on the third floor. The library, which was two rooms combined, was also on the third floor. The fourth floor housed the fourth and the fifth-grade classes, the two bilingual Modified Instructional Service I class and one monolingual M.I.S. I class. There was a science room on the fourth floor also. There were two cluster teachers who ran a science program from that room. They kept some small animals there and charts depicting topics being taught were displayed on the walls.

The structure of the building was an old one. Still, it seemed to be in good shape. It had not been painted professionally for many years, but the custodian had paid some of the cleaning men to paint parts of the school. Other schools in the district had been painted by contracted agencies. The school, however, had competent people who cleaned, and it never looked dirty or unkempt.

The real problem in the maintenance of the school was the heating. During the winter season the school went virtually unheated for many days. These occurrences were usually after a weekend or a holiday break. The head custodian always had some lame excuse for not providing proper heat. He always said that it was the structure of the building that did not allow heat to reach certain classrooms. Otherwise, he said that the thermometers were not working. Maria wondered if he was stealing the money for fuel. Other teachers told her that there were no problems with heat before the previous custodian retired.

The community was very diverse ethnically. Although there are American-born families whose children attended the school, most of the population were foreign born. Most of the children were born in other countries or were first generation American. The school was almost entirely African American and Hispanic. There was one white child. He was a boy enrolled in a monolingual M.I.S. IV class. The M.I.S. IV class is a class for young children ages 5.9 to 7.8 who need extra help to succeed in school.

The M.I.S. I class was for older children from age 7.8 all the way through high school if the service was needed. Most of the residents of this community received some form of public assistance. Some of the mothers worked as home attendants or in factories in Manhattan. Incomes are very low for the most part. Many households were single parent households in which the head of the house was the mother. Sometimes the mother was twenty-one or twenty-two years old. Most families had large numbers of children-four, five, six. One of Maria's students came from a family of ten children.

The housing in the community consisted almost entirely of big buildings. There was a large public housing in which many of the students lived. Parents complained often of bad housing conditions. The people who lived in privately-owned buildings complained about lack of heat, hot water, and broken doors which allowed easy access to the dwellings. The parents who lived in the public housing project complained about drug trafficking, lack of security, and a high crime wave which prevented them from going out at night or even just after dark. Many were afraid to let their children out alone even in the daytime.

Maria liked the ethnic diversity among her new colleagues also. Most of the teachers were women of color. There was many black women teachers and two black men teachers. There were six white women teachers and two white men teachers. There were fourteen Hispanic women teachers-seven were Puerto Rican, five were Dominican, one was Ecuadorian, and one was from El Salvador. There were three Puerto Rican men teachers.

The parents were not involved in the mechanics of the school to any great extent. There was a P.T.A. which assisted the school with fund-raising activities and school pictures. One of the parents sat in on the Pupil- Personnel Committee meetings. Many of the children commute to school from the West Side of the district which may be one reason for lack of parent involvement.

However, even the parents who lived near the school barely participated in school functions. The P.T.A. consisted of about three active members. The parents on the Pupil Personnel Committee were consistent. Most of the children enrolled in Special Education classes were brought by bus.

Many of the kindergarten children in regular education were also brought by bus. They lived in the zone for another school which was over-crowded. Therefore, they came to this school.

The bilingual classes were all Spanish-English and all the children in them were Hispanic. There were absolutely no exceptions. The monolingual classes had mixed Hispanic and Black populations, but the Black children were a majority in the monolingual classes.

Maria observed one big problem which bothered her immensely. The problem was one of discipline. Although there was little fighting among the children, many of the teachers seemed to have a very hard time maintaining discipline. At times, children ran wildly in the hallways and on the stairs. It was not unusual for children to curse at teachers, and even the principal had received her fair share of bad language from some children. Maria vowed to teach her students how to show respect. She would teach first by her example. She decided she would maintain a professional and courteous demeanor so that the children would emulate her.

The curriculum was basically the same as in most schools—the basic subjects were Reading, Mathematics, Social Studies, Science, and Writing. Art and Music were taught independently by two cluster teachers. The children went to a computer class every day. There they did Reading and Mathematics skills. In theory, everything was in place academically. However, when the Reading scores were published, this school showed only ten per cent of the children reading at grade level. This was a shame and a nightmare for any school anywhere in the world. The fact that it would happen in one of the richest and most powerful countries in the world was astounding. Maria vowed to make a positive difference in the lives of her students.

At home, Orlando laughed because he didn't believe that anyone could change a school like that. Dona Angelica worried about the safety of her only child. Baby Angie smiled gleefully and played with her Raggedy Anne doll as her parents talked.

Maria was happy to have been assigned to this school. It was the poorest community she had ever seen. When she was growing up with Amanda, Elaine, and Carmen they had also been poor. But their parents all worked and there was always food and shelter. It was a given. Maria had never gone without a meal. She always had decent, if not expensive, clothes. She went to Catholic school, and she had always had a home. She now worked with children who had spent time in homeless shelters. Several of the mothers were battered wives. Some of the children's parents had been in jail for drugs and other offenses. Maria loved her students. She was assigned to a bilingual M.I.S. IV class. She had ten children in her class and a paraprofessional to help her. The para was a middle-aged woman named Gloria Gonzalez. She was also Puerto Rican. Mrs. Gonzalez had very good work ethics. She was very serious about her job. When she saw Maria, she liked her instantly. Gloria has been a para at the school for nineteen years. She had worked with some of the most experienced teachers. Maria knew that she could learn from Gloria even if she was the teacher and Gloria, was the para. Together they made an outstanding team.

Maria learned from Gloria that she could not react to everything. She had to focus on her students, her classroom management skills, and her relationship with the parents of her students.

There were many problems. There were many perplexities in the school and in the community. Maria did everything she could to familiarize herself with her new environment. Still, she couldn't help worrying about the conditions she observed.

Although there was a very high bilingual population, there are no books in Spanish. The librarian was a charming lady who got along very well with the children and seemed to care very much. She read stories to the younger children and helped the older children choose books. She held book sales and coordinated specials on books in conjunction with the book companies. This library and its librarian were bright spots in the school. However, when Maria entered the library, she saw that there were no books over a third-grade reading level. When she asked the librarian about this, the woman answered that if she ordered books over a third-grade reading level none of the children could read them. She also informed Maria that the principal would not buy books in Spanish.

There was a science room in the school. This was really a cluster position which was run by two former classroom teachers. One of them had her state certification in supervision and administration. Classroom teachers brought their classes here and left them with these two teachers. The children received a lesson which usually culminated with some hands-on activity. The children also got to ask questions and work in small groups. Unfortunately, only the older children were able to take this class which was a shame because there was very little Science being taught in the younger grades. Maria observed these two Science teachers and structured lesson plans in science like theirs, but with topics appropriate for the age ranges of her students.

There was no gymnasium in the school. There was no real gym teacher either. A former classroom teacher taught gym. The gym classes were conducted in what used to be the cold lunchroom or the yard. The cold lunchroom was a space on the first floor right outside the present lunchroom. It was near the security guard's desk.

There was one principal and two assistant principals. There was no position for a bilingual coordinator, but a bilingual M.I.S1 teacher held the title. She was Puerto Rican. A bilingual paraprofessional oversaw administering the L.A.B. test. This test, the Language Accessory Battery, determines if a student is entitled to bilingual services or not. Those who pass it go into monolingual (English only) classes while those who fail it are placed in bilingual classes. The English test is given each year to every student until he/she passes it. Some students never do. Others pass it the first time they take it.

There were two assistant principals. One oversaw kindergarten through second grade. The other oversaw third grade through the fifth grade. The Special Education classes were included in this line. The assistant principal for the lower grades supervised the M.I.S. IV classes for younger children, while the other one supervised the M.I.S1 classes for older children.

Maria used all the materials that the school supplied as well as the some that she bought herself. She bought Phonics books because she believed that that was the best methodology to teach Reading in the primary grades. All her students had some sort of handicapping condition.

Most of them were learning disabled. A few had speech impairments and one was mildly retarded. Maria never looked on them as handicapped students. She saw them as her students. She was honored to be their teacher and she worked exceedingly hard. She only missed one day of work during her first year of teaching because little Angie was sick.

Carmen becomes a banker.

Boston is the oldest city in the United States except for St. Augustine in Florida. It is a city that played an important part in the history of the United States. The architecture is a reminder of America's past. A tourist can still see Paul Revere's house and the ship from which the Boston Tea Party was held. The population of Boston is now much more diverse and different ethnic groups are "accepted".

The world of banking and finance has always been a ruthless one. Only the strongest survive. There are bankers who would sell both their parents if the sale would increase their profit margins. Despite that, Boston's banking industry was not ready for Carmen Cortez. Carmen graduated from Boston University's School of Management. She continued studying for her M.B.A. at Boston University. Her aunt, Mercedes, her legal guardian, worked at Boston University. Therefore, tuition was free.

Carmen's brother, Fernando, had taken the ROTC program and had graduated as a second lieutenant. He was now a career soldier. Carmen was home in Mercedes' house. She had never married or established serious relationships. While still in her early twenties, she was appointed a branch manager in one of the most prestigious banks in Boston. This was partly because of her excellent credentials and partly because of her dedication to hard work. The bank wanted someone who would devote most of his/her life to making profits. She was feared but not liked by those whom she supervised. One day, she passed by two tellers and heard:

"Where's that Puerto Rican bitch?" asked one teller.

"I don't know. I saw her pass by a little while ago." answered the other.

Carmen passed by the tellers' booths nonchalantly pretending that she hadn't heard. She counted the money in their cash boxes without looking at or greeting either one of the condescending tellers. They smiled politely as if they hadn't said anything. After all, Carmen was their boss. Carmen finished and went to her desk on the platform. The doors opened at 9 O'clock, and customers would be streaming in.

Carmen made no effort to be popular. She had a job to do, and she did it. Luckily, she was good at her job. She brought many customers to the bank. She attracted many Spanish speaking investors from all the different countries in the Spanish Caribbean and South America. Her decisions about financing and loans to corporations had always been sound ones. The bank had never lost money. Her decisions on hiring and firing personnel were always logical. A valuable employee was never let go and a lethargic one was never retained. Carmen used her brains in her job not her heart or her emotions.

This was the right way to do things in banking. Carmen did not work in a hospital like Amanda and Elaine or a school like Maria. Banks existed to make money. That was the bottom line. People who studied banking and finance did so to make money. What Carmen hadn't realized was that all the money and material belongings would not eradicate the agony that burned within her. By the end of the day, Carmen decided that the bank did not need so many tellers. Two of them were given their pink slips that evening.

The bank invested heavily in real estate. Boston is a very desirable town to live in. Over 250,000 students a year converge there. Many lived off the campuses of their respective colleges and paid high rents in private buildings. Many investors took advantage of this opportunity to make money. Carmen scrutinized the loan applications and made decisions whether to grant them loans.

There was a poor part of Massachusetts called Jamaica Plains which was inhabited by many indigent Hispanic families who had migrated to Boston from other parts of the United States looking for work. Some had set up small businesses which catered to other Hispanics in their burgh. The community established in Jamaica Plain resembled that of Bergen Street in Brooklyn. However, with the crunch for property, investors were also looking to buy land in this area. The students, for the most part, did not mind living in a predominantly Hispanic area.

One of Carmen's customers applied for a loan to buy a building in the heart of Jamaica Plain. Carmen, being as thorough as she was, decided that she should go look at the property with the bank's building inspector. She would meet him there. This observation would help her decide whether to grant the loan. She didn't want to spend the bank's money on a property which no one would want to live in.

The ride from Commonwealth Avenue was breathtaking. Carmen had hated having to leave New York so abruptly, but one comforting aspect of Boston had always been the scenery. Massachusetts must be one of the most beautiful states in the United States especially the countryside-the suburban and rural areas. Jamaica Plain was not a suburban area, but Carmen passed many lovely places before arriving there.

The building was in good condition. The exterior appeared to be free of imperfection. Carmen wondered how many college students would live this far from most of the college campuses. However, the building would make a good rental for families and students who graduated and wanted to remain in Boston. The neighborhood, although not elegant, was certainly livable. There was a small Hispanic grocery store on the first floor. These were known in New York as "bodegas". It was run by a Puerto Rican couple who had lived in New York for several years. When Carmen arrived, the bank inspector was already waiting for her in front of the building. He said that he had been observing the neighborhood and its residents and so far, found it to be good. He wanted to check the inside structure, the electricity, and the plumbing with her present. They proceeded upstairs. The residents of the building gave Carmen unfriendly looks. They answered her questions in a polite but cold manner.

The apartments were all in good form. It was a five-story building with four two-bedroom apartments on each floor except the first floor where the store was located. The apartments facing the front paid a ten percent higher rent than those facing the back. A total of five dwellings were vacant. The present owner was keeping some units empty in hopes of making the building more desirable for sale. He was right. The potential new owner wanted the entire building vacant so that he could renovate the building and raise the rents. All the tenants had been notified of a possible eviction or a huge rent increase. The applicant had not informed Carmen of this. Carmen finally reached the bodega on the first floor. She entered the store and observed the proprietor. The woman wore a denim jumper with a white cotton blouse underneath. She measured barely five feet in her walking shoes. Her clothes were modest but immaculate. As Carmen entered the store, Rosa Padilla was waiting on a customer. The store was clean and neat additionally. The signs advertising the prices and specials were neatly written in both Spanish and English. Rosa treated her customer with courtesy and respect. The customer responded kindly.

When the customer left, Carmen introduced herself to the owner. She informed her that she was the bank official who would have the ultimate say on whether the applicant would get the mortgage.

"So, you are the lady who is going to throw us all out onto the street!" said Rosa, as calmly as she could.

"What?" asked Carmen, as politely as *she* could.

"People apply to my bank for loans every day. Some people get them and some people don't. It's as simple as that." informed Carmen.

"It is very simple indeed. When the new owner ejects me from this building, how simple will it be for me to find another store? How simple will it be for me to earn a living? I guess that I could clean houses or wash dishes in a restaurant. That is simple, isn't it?" continued Rosa.

Carmen didn't know what to say. She stared at the woman who reminded her of someone—another hard-working bodegera—Emilia Ramos. Tears swelled in her eyes for the first time since her parents died. Rosa continued talking, but Carmen could barely hear her anymore. She had gone back in time emotionally to another era of her life. She was immersed in her daydream.

"I provide quality merchandise at reasonable prices. I give credit to neighbors in need. I have been here ten years. Now I am almost out because some greedy investor thinks to throw me and all the tenants upstairs out. Where are they going to go? Did the bank think of that?" inquired Rosa.

"No. They didn't think about any of you and neither did I." said Carmen "We are not social workers. We are not running a charitable agency. The bank is in business to make money. The investor is in business to make money."

"It is unfortunate that sometimes people must get hurt." replied Carmen honestly.

Rosa Padilla gazed at her in amazement. She glared at her high class clothes. Rosa would have to work a month to buy the dress Carmen wore.

She'd have to work another month on the shoes and handbag. Yet, this woman stood in her humble store and lectured her on the realities of banking.

"When some people need or want to acquire more wealth, they often trample all over people's lives. I, however, will not allow you or the people upstairs to get hurt." stated Carmen.

Now, Rosa was totally confused. The woman who came to examine the building for the new buyer was guaranteeing her safety. The present land-lord and the new prospective landlord had both written to the tenants informing them that they would have to leave. Who was this young woman? How could she ensure the security and interest of the inhabitants? Rosa wondered.

"What part of Puerto Rico are you from?" asked Carmen sincerely.

"Aguadillas". answered Rosa.

"I lived in New York until I was sixteen years old. Then I came to live in Boston with my aunt when my parents died." said Carmen.

"I want some Mavi and one of those dulce de leche before I leave. You will not be evicted. Here is my card if you have any questions." said Carmen as she exited the store.

Carmen returned to her office and called her district manager. She asked about the legalities of rejecting the customer's application for a loan. The district manager liked Carmen and told her to find a qualified reason. She informed her boss that she wanted to turn down this man's request and buy the building herself—all cash. She would not ask the bank for a mortgage. She would use the funds she received from the sale of her house in Brooklyn and her parents' life insurance policies. Carmen convinced him that it would not look good for the bank to evict poor people. If the media got a hold of this story, the bank could lose many potential investors. Carmen did not tell her superior that *she* would contact the media if this deal did not go her way. Her district manager approved. Carmen dictated a very carefully worded letter to the mortgage applicant explaining why the bank could not approve his request for a loan to that particular property. Then she contacted the present owner by phone and made him a cash offer. He readily agreed because he would have his money within two weeks.

Carmen now had a sound investment as well as a warm feeling in her heart. She hadn't felt this good in years. After purchasing the building, she hired a superintendent to clean and repair the building. He reported directly to her on the developments every afternoon. She also gave her home and work numbers to Rosa Padilla so that she could call and let Carmen know if the superintendent was doing his job. Carmen believed in double insurance. The tenants paid reasonable rents and most of them paid on time. The five vacant apartments were leased at market value (not a penny higher) to families recommended by some of the present tenants. Carmen and Rosa Padilla became friendly. Carmen felt that she had just bought back a part of her past. She had bought back a part of Bergen Street and Emilia Ramos.

The Girls of Bergen Street Move On

Bergen Street itself was evolving. The girls had all moved away. Carmen lived in Boston. Maria lived in Queens. Amanda was at the Columbia Medical School in Washington Heights and lived there. Elaine lived in

Park Slope in the home Domingo had now inherited. The neighborhood was becoming more and more costly to live in. Several of the buildings had been turned into condominiums and many of the former residents had been priced out. Gowanus Park remained the same because it was located within the projects.

Miranda sadly packed her belongings into the big boxes Elaine had sent over. There were so many memories. The projects were governed by city laws. Miranda no longer qualified for the apartment because all her children were married and gone. Elaine's in-laws had gone back to Puerto Rico and given the house to Domingo and Elaine. Miranda and Guillermo were moving into Elaine's house. This was better than being "transferred" to a smaller apartment by the city. They'd rent the upper floor from Elaine. Miranda would take care of little Carmen because Elaine wanted to go back to work. Miranda thought that she was tired of this apartment and of the projects. However, packing all her cherished belongings, which included some old toys and clothes that the children had left behind, was a bittersweet mission.

Lourdes and Miguel Martinez still lived on Bergen Street. Lourdes felt very lonely without Amanda in the apartment. Their building was governed by the rent control laws and they were in no danger of losing their apartment. The parents were so proud of their daughter. Amanda barely had time to come and see them. Every weekend they drove up to her dorm in Washington Heights.

They'd have dinner together in a Dominican restaurant every Saturday. Amanda worked so hard, and she was doing so well. She was in her senior year of medical school and would be doing her internship the following year. After that, Amanda explained she'd do her residency. Then finally she'd be a doctor.

Dona Angelica was getting used to living in Queens. Orlando had given the superintendent a big tip to reserve the small apartment in front of Maria's. There was a large Hispanic community in Queens. There were some Puerto Ricans but most of the residents were from Colombia, Ecuador,

Peru, and Brazil. A little further up there was a Dominican com- munity. Dona Angelica made friends there.

Maria worked so hard. She taught Special Education students and was responsible for teaching all the basic skills in both English and Spanish. Dona Angelica felt that teaching all those skills in one language would have been enough. Orlando got a job as a gym teacher in a high school in Manhattan. Maria stayed in her school in the Bronx. They saved and looked for high interest-bearing accounts. They wanted to buy a house of their own—just a little house. But at least it would be theirs. Finally, Maria found one in the newspapers that was advertised as below market value. They had a hard time getting a mortgage, but finally they were approved. The house was one hundred years old—the oldest one on the block. It was in Astoria Heights. The size was just about adequate. There was a living room, and a large eat—in kitchen on the first floor. Three bedrooms occupied the second floor—a large master bedroom, and two small rooms. There was also a basement and a large backyard. Dona Angelica and little Angie would each get one of the small bedrooms. Dona Angelica could store her leftover furniture in the basement. The grandmother was delighted at the prospect of not paying rent.

At the same time, Amanda labored and labored. She was so close to accomplishing her vision. She socialized very little. Throughout her years at college, she had dated here and there but she had not fallen in love. Amanda hadn't even spoken to Maria since Angie had been born. That was about two years ago.

She knew Maria taught in the South Bronx and Elaine worked in a neighborhood hospital in Brooklyn, but she didn't really communicate with them anymore. She needed to focus.

The moment Amanda stepped into the hospital, she felt at home. She was where she wanted to be. She shadowed an experienced doctor and learned from him. Her area of specialty was pediatrics. He was tall, handsome, and very fair. Amanda thought he was just about the lightest person she had ever seen. When she was a child, she and the other girls used to tease

Elaine about being so white. Dr. Fitzpatrick was young and energetic. He was hard-working and sensitive, and he treated parents and children with respect. The hospital housed a low-income clinic. Some patients paid on a sliding scale, some had Medicaid, and some paid nothing at all.

The two doctors worked side by side. They spent countless hours together discussing patients, going through files, and making decisions for further treatment. Amanda knew that she had found the man she could love. At first, she tried to resist the feelings. She endeavored to focus. But it was all ineffective.

She had indeed fallen in love for the very first time. Someone was as important to her as her profession. Amanda didn't know what to do about it. Dr. Harold Fitzpatrick didn't know and didn't notice. He was proper and correct in his dealings with Amanda. He treated her as a professional and a colleague. She responded in kind outwardly.

One day, he asked her to have dinner with him as they left the clinic. She readily agreed, trying not to sound too anxious. After that date, they went out casually. Amanda finished her internship and received a raving evaluation from him. She was quickly accepted for residency at the same hospital.

One quiet night, she worked late. As she left one of the children' rooms, Harold suddenly appeared. She asked him to wait for her in the cafeteria; she had not finished her shift. She went down as soon as she could. He smiled softly as she approached his table.

Amanda Gets Married

"We worked well, together, didn't we?" said Harold."

Yes, I guess we did." answered Amanda nervously.

"We got along well too." stated Harold calmly. Her nervousness made him smile a little wider.

"Yeah." Amanda answered. That was all she could say. "Want to get married?" asked Harold quietly.

"Sure. When?" asked Amanda, not realizing what she had just said. "This weekend. We can go to a chapel in Las Vegas or somewhere. Anywhere where our parents can't bother us." said Harold.

Harold explained that he had told his parents about Amanda and that they vehemently opposed the marriage. They were first generation Irish-American and they did not approve of her natural tan. They wanted their grandchildren to be all Irish. Harold had decided to ignore their request and follow his heart.

Amanda and Harold were married in Las Vegas on May 30, 1980. They moved into Harold's Fifth Avenue apartment overlooking Central Park. Harold laughed and said that when Amanda started working, they would move into the penthouse. Lourdes and Miguel Martinez were shocked. They didn't know whether to be happy for their daughter or to be upset with her for not telling them about her wedding. Either way, they reconciled with the fact that their daughter was married and wished her well. They prayed for her happiness.

Harold's parents, on the other hand, cursed the day of their son's union and hoped for a speedy separation. Amanda tried to ignore their coldness. She was determined not to let them win.

Amanda finished her residency and was appointed to the hospital as a staff pediatrician. Harold worked there too, but they decided to take different shifts. They started private practices separately also so that their home life would not interfere with their professional life. Amanda's office was situated around the part of Manhattan known as Spanish Harlem and affectionately called "El Barrio". Her patients were mostly poor children whose families relied on Medicaid and other types of insurance.

Amanda also established a sliding scale billing practice for families whose incomes were low but did not have Medicaid. Most of her patients were Hispanic. Amanda had never been happier.

Chapter Five

Personal lives

One never leaves the place where one was born no matter how many miles one travels. The further we go from our roots, our heritage, the closer we get to it. Is that not true? It was for the girls from Bergen Street. They just didn't know it yet.

The years appeared to stand still for Maria. Each day at work was like the first day. Her students completed their M.I.S. IV program (which lasted three years) and graduated to general education or a higher functioning special education class. A new class came. Maria became a part of her school community. She got to know many of the parents even on a first name basis. She often taught siblings. Sometimes one child would graduate, and his brother or sister would enter her class the next fall. Her hard work and enthusiasm were readily recognized by the principal.

She loved the children, and they sensed it. There were many expressions of their mutual affection. One day, Maria went down to pick up her students after lunch. Several of her boys were running around the lunch- room unsupervised. Of course, the school aide should have been there, but she wasn't. Still the children should know the proper behavior by now. Maria quickly ran to her class. She yelled for the boys to sit down at the table.

She looked up at the one who was slower coming down and yelled again. Nelson, the little boy looked up at her and said:

"Don't yell at me, Mrs. Rodriguez. I know you like me.'

Many of the parents were equally impressed with Maria's teaching methods and classroom management skills. They admired the way she handled her class of handicapped students and got them to learn. Her reputation proceeded by word of mouth. Parents recommended her to other parents. The district office received several requests to place children in her class.

However, Maria noted sadly that Orlando was becoming somewhat distant in his attitude towards her. She didn't know why and had trouble finding the right words to ask him. He was a gym teacher and was doing well in his profession. He had not gone on to study for his Masters' degree as Maria had done. The little house was good for the family. Angie had started first grade in Catholic School. Maria placed her daughter in Catholic School because of religious reasons. The public schools were not allowed to teach religion. He came home, had dinner, watched television and went to sleep. Maria didn't know that he began to resent the personal calls from parents to her. He felt that the time she spent talking to parents, whom she saw every day, could be spent talking to him. But he could not convince Maria of that. When Maria was not talking to parents, she was helping Angie with her homework, or she was taking her mother to the doctor. Dona Angelica's health was failing. She had been diagnosed with diabetes and heart problems. Orlando seemed to have no place in her life. It was just so hard to get Maria's attention. It appeared that the lines of communication between the husband and wife had closed. Dona Angelica's health continued to deteriorate.

"This is our house, grandma." said Angie.

"Is it, baby? So, it is." replied Dona Angelica.

Angie smiled seeing that her grandmother almost forgot where they lived. Her grandmother picked her up at school every day but sometimes she seemed incoherent. She'd come late and stand in the wrong corner. Angie was seven years old and didn't take much notice. She loved her grandmother and that was all she needed to know. Other parents, who knew Dona Angelica, often directed her. People thought that Dona Angelica was getting on in years and was just forgetting things.

Maria began to worry more and more. Finally, on a hunch, she hired a neighbor woman to come to the house every day and help her mother. The woman took Angie to school and stayed with Dona Angelica until Maria came home. Orlando approved because this gave him and Maria more time to talk. Maria told her mother that the lady was there to "help" her not take care of her.

While Maria struggled with her challenges, Amanda worked with a fiery at the clinic. There were always so many patients. Poor people appeared to have more offspring than middle class or rich people. There was no shortage of children to see ever. But while tending to other people's children, Dr. Martinez-Fitzpatrick realized that she was going to have a little person of her own. Amanda was overjoyed. Her parents were elated to have a grandchild even if they hardly knew the father. Harold's response was lukewarm.

"Wow, so quickly." said Harold.

"We've been married two years." responded Amanda.

"So, we have. Good years too." said Harold smiling.

"Good years. "Agreed Amanda feeling uneasy.

"I guess our child will be lighter than you and darker than me." said Harold slowly.

"I guess. I hope that it's not a problem" answered Amanda, hurt by the comment.

Harold smiled slightly and said that he was happy. He hoped that it would be a boy. Amanda smiled too knowing that Harold had reservations about bringing a child into the world who wasn't going to look just like him. He married an olive toned Puerto Rican woman and he expected to have white children. At this moment, she saw her husband in a different light.

They had never actually discussed having children. Amanda started feeling that he might love her, but not want to have a child with her.

Harold Michael Fitzpatrick was born weighing seven pounds, fifteen ounces on May 31, 1983. His middle name "Michael" was for Amanda's father, Miguel. Michael is the English version of Miguel. He was the most beautiful baby Amanda had ever seen. That was her objective opinion. Amanda decided to take a maternity leave to take care of him. Lourdes and Miguel were the proudest of grandparents. They had always avoided visiting Amanda in her penthouse apartment, but now that the baby was born that would change. Harold's parents didn't bother to come and visit. They had no interest in the baby.

Maria, Orlando, and Angie made the trip to Manhattan to see the baby. Elaine, Domingo, and little Carmen came as well. All brought gifts for Amanda's baby.

"How much do they make exactly?" inquired Orlando, thinking aloud.

"Hundreds of thousands a year. But Amanda has never bragged about it." answered Maria.

"She doesn't have to." Orlando said. "This place speaks for itself."

Elaine sighed as she entered the building. She really didn't know what to say.

"Good thing, Amanda didn't marry an auto mechanic. She wouldn't live here." said Domingo, pretending to joke.

"She wasn't as lucky as me. I have the best husband and the best house in the world." answered Elaine sincerely.

The doorman treated them as if they were royalty. He knew that Dr. and Dr. Fitzpatrick were expecting them. He addressed them as "Mr. and Mrs. Rodriguez," and "Mr. and Mrs. Perez" and their young daughters. Little Carmen held Angie's hand in the elevator. Both girls giggled. Carmen was two years older, and Angie loved playing with her.

Amanda was at the door of her apartment when the group arrived upstairs. She was thrilled to see them all again. It had been a while since they had spent time together. Seeing them all come off the elevator together gave her a warm feeling. She almost felt homesick for her familiar environment.

The housekeeper came running to take everyone's coats. She put them all away within seconds. Amanda ushered them into the most capacious living room any of them had ever seen. Maria and Elaine had never been to Amanda's house before. They were awed by the furniture, the rugs, and the adornments. The children started to run and hide between the divans. Maria quickly clasped them both and sat them down. This made the girls laugh again.

Amanda brought out the baby and showed him first to the little girls. "Do you girls want to see my baby?" asked Amanda.

"Yeah." answered both simultaneously.

"Well, here he is." said Amanda. She was delighted to show her child.

All the guests smiled broadly when they saw the baby. They gave Amanda the gifts they had brought. Maria held the baby for the longest period. Harold came out of the bedroom presently and everyone congratulated him. He smiled to a degree and was decorous to everyone. Maria and Elaine attributed his mannerisms to his not being "latino". They didn't expect him to hug or shake hands with anyone. "Gringos" were distant compared to Hispanics.

The dining room was elegant. Neither Maria nor Elaine had dining rooms in their houses and this was a new experience. As he sat at the huge dinner table in this exquisite chamber, Orlando thought about how hard he and Maria had worked together to buy their modest house. He knew that Maria loved their dwelling and would probably not trade it for this residence. Still, he was sorry that he could not afford a place like this one.

Domingo was quiet throughout the meal. He didn't seem to have much to say except to the children. He kept passing them things and helping them with their food. He tried not to look at Harold. Domingo instantly disliked him, but he was a guest in this house, and he wanted to be gracious. Domingo, like Orlando, felt inadequate because he could not afford a house like this one. He had always thought that his house was so splendid, and it was in their Brooklyn neighborhood. It was the most elegant abode in the area.

Luckily, the women did all the talking. They had so much to catch up on. Sometimes they appeared to be talking at the same time. Amanda, Maria, and Elaine discussed their different experiences throughout the years. It was almost like when they were children.

"I've worked in Special Education since I got my master's degree. I teach the Modified Instructions IV program in the South Bronx. My children age from 5.9 years old to 7.9 years old. My class is for early intervention for children who have some sort of handicapping condition." said Maria proudly.

Harold rolled his eyes not understanding what Maria had to be so proud of. Most people wouldn't even want to go into that neighborhood. He felt that most people wouldn't even want to work with children who were handicapped, at least not on an ongoing basis. It was different to see them occasionally. As a doctor he took care of children who were sick, but he didn't have to deal with them and their parents daily. Besides, the practice that he established was geared to middle class and upper middle-class children who came in clean and well fed.

"Many of my students go on to regular education classes after my class." continued Maria triumphantly.

Maria did not notice Harold shrug, but Domingo and Orlando did. They didn't say anything. But they had a hard time controlling their indignation. Orlando listened to his wife and realized what he should have realized all along. She was a born teacher, and she was sent to this earth to work with disabled children. It seemed as if he was understanding her enthusiasm for the first time. She loved her students, and they loved her back. She must have tried to explain it to him a million times, but he hadn't comprehended her. Hearing her speak to her childhood friends in this exquisite dining room, everything became clear to him. He and Maria would talk at home later. He would endeavor to open the lines of communication again. It wasn't that Maria was neglecting him or Angie, it was that she had a mission.

Harold turned to Domingo and asked him what he did for a living. Domingo did not particularly want to speak to Harold, but he couldn't decline to answer.

"I am an auto mechanic. I own my own auto repair shop." stated Domingo flatly.

"I'll keep you in mind when I have a fender bender." joked Harold.

"No, I don't do body work on cars. I repair engines." corrected Domingo.

"You didn't have to go to college to repair cars." said Harold.

"No, but I had to go to a professional school." stated Domingo proudly.

"Do you work long hours? Is it hard work?" asked Harold with feigned alacrity.

"Yes, it is. But I love what I do just like Maria does. I am my own boss. I set the standards in my shop and no one tells me what to do." said Domingo.

At this point, Elaine cut into the conversation. She told Harold how Domingo had five employees and owned his shop free and clear. She knew that Harold had been trying to put down her husband, so she clarified a few things for him. She told everyone how they owned a two-family house and her parents lived upstairs. Domingo had made all this possible. Their daughter, Carmen, was attending a private parochial school which was very exclusive. Neither the house nor the shop was leveraged.

"I work as a licensed practical nurse in Long Island College Hospital. I work in the geriatric ward. As an LPN, I do mostly hand on, bedside manner, labor." said Elaine proudly.

Harold saw an LPN (who was not even registered nurse) as one step below the maintenance man. The maintenance people had a better union and made more money. Harold started to realize how he had married a woman whose culture and background were so different from his own.

When he met Amanda at the hospital, he saw her individually. He beheld only a medical student who was graduating from one of the best medical schools in the country. After meeting her friends, he understood why she insisted on working in a clinic in East Harlem and attending to only poor children. Why wouldn't she? She felt close to them.

After dinner, the group moved into the parlor for coffee and dessert. The living room was just as stunning as the dining room. Amanda got the baby and held him in her arms to the delight of the two little girls. He was handsome with his sandy hair and big hazel eyes. Amanda passed him to Maria. After the maid picked up the dishes from the cake and coffee, Domingo announced that he was tired, and he had to get up early in the morning. Elaine protested only mildly. She had been married almost ten years and understood her husband very well. She knew that Domingo could not put up with Harold any longer and stayed this long only out of courtesy to Amanda. Domingo, Elaine, and Carmen left.

Maria stayed behind a little longer. She was grateful for this time to talk to Amanda alone.

"You know who's been asking about you?" asked Maria, smiling.

"No, who?" asked Amanda honestly.

"Carmen" answered Maria still grinning.

"She's been asking for several months. I gave her your address and telephone number so that she could get in touch with you, but she said that she'd rather hear from me.

What does that mean?" asked Maria.

"I don't know. There's certainly no reason why I wouldn't talk to her." replied to Amanda.

"Let's call her from here. She only lives in Boston. This way, we'll clear the air." said Maria.

"Okay" agreed Amanda.

Amanda had not really spoken to Carmen since her parents died. She spoke briefly and superficially at Elaine's wedding and then Carmen left abruptly. Losing Carmen's friendship had left Amanda with an empty feeling. Maria had the right idea in wanting to call her. When Carmen answered, Amanda's heart beat faster.

"Hello." said Carmen, not sounding particularly interested.

"Hello, Carmen?" asked Amanda.

"Yes, this is Carmen. Who's speaking?" inquired Carmen. "Amanda" Amanda informed her.

There was silence on the other end. Then Amanda rekindled the conversation.

"I'm calling you from my apartment in Manhattan. Maria is here with me, and Elaine and her family have just left. Maria suggested we call you together and chat for a while." continued Amanda.

"I'm glad you called. It's so wonderful to hear your voice." said Carmen.

"Yours, too. agreed Amanda.

Amanda told Carmen about her husband and her baby. She apprised her of her work in the clinic in East Harlem. Carmen nodded as Amanda spoke. She was not at all surprised that Amanda had dedicated her life to curing poor children. Carmen congratulated her on her marriage and the birth of her baby. Her words sounded sincere.

Carmen told Amanda about her work at the bank. She was the branch manager and had made a lot of good deals for the bank. However, the deal she was most proud of was the one she made for herself. She told Amanda about how she had gone to inspect a building on behalf of the bank and decided to buy it instead of letting the tenants get evicted. Carmen laughed quietly as she described the bodegera who ran the store on the first floor. She reminded her so much of Emilia Ramos. When she met her, she couldn't go through with the deal.

Amanda smiled. She was so pleased to know that Carmen, despite her tough exterior was genuinely a humanitarian deep down inside.

"I feel so good when I go and visit my building." said Carmen.

"Are you making any money on it or just breaking even?" asked Amanda.

"I am making money. I bought it with cash from my parents' home and their life insurance policies. The rent I collect maintains the building and gives me cash flow. That investment helps ensure my retirement also." said Carmen.

"Thinking about retirement so soon, Carmen, really?" joked Amanda.

"A person must. It's important or we end up little old people who depend on social services and welfare to get by "explained Carmen.

"I'm going to have to talk to you about developing a retirement plan for myself. It's great to have a friend who is a financial wizard." answered Amanda sincerely.

Amanda had never thought about saving for retirement.

Carmen had always been very practical and levelheaded. She was never frivolous even when she was an adolescent. Amanda always wondered how she was able to cope with the tragic death of her parents and still go on to live such a productive life. Amanda sensed a sadness in Carmen's voice.

"How is your aunt Mercedes?" inquired Amanda.

"She's fine. I still live with her." answered Carmen.

"I'll never forget that street fight with Emilia Ramos." said Amanda.

"Yes, she gave a bad impression that day. But she was really a good person. She's been a second mother to me and Fernando. She did everything for us and she never asked for anything in return. She never touched any of the money our parents left. She hasn't accepted anything even when we offered it. She told us that she wanted us to hold our resources for our future." said Carmen.

"Still, when I think back, I feel that she could have worked matters out more amicably with Emilia. She didn't have to threaten her with lawyers and make a scene in the street." continued Carmen.

"The Ramos family went back to Puerto Rico, you know. said Amanda.

"I know, I still write to them. The bonds have never been broken." said Carmen to Amanda's surprise.

"Carmen let's get together soon, all four of us." said Amanda.

"Sure. That'll be great." responded Carmen.

"Talk to you soon." said Amanda.

"I'll be looking forward to hearing from you." said Carmen.

Maria could barely conceal her delight. Carmen and Amanda were talking again and that made her immensely happy. She never could under- stand the impasse between them, but she was glad they were mending their relationship. Orlando was in the den with Harold watching a news program. Angie was asleep on the chaise in the living room. Maria took the opportunity to ask Amanda why her friendship with Carmen had become strained. Carmen blushed but decided to tell Maria anyway.

"It was a long time ago. We were still in high school. I was saddened at not being able to go to a private or parochial high school like you, Elaine, and Carmen. Carmen and I were just hanging out in Gowanus Park which was always our favorite place to talk. Remember how comfortable and at ease we always felt there? Maria nodded. I was feeling particularly bad one day and I went to the park. Carmen was passing by, and she stayed with me. I had had a bad day at school. There had been another fight with that Martha Williams. I told her about it. She wanted to go down and fight Martha for me. I laughed that off, of course. We walked over to her house for some refreshments. While we were there, she hugged me and tried to kiss me in a romantic way. Carmen is gay. I don't know if she still is, or if that was just a passing thing, but that's what happened that day. I implored her to keep the occurrence a secret. She did. We barely spoke after that." related Carmen.

"I won't say anything to anyone." promised Maria.

"Then her parents died in that tragic accident." continued Amanda.

"Afterwards, she moved to Boston with her aunt." added Maria.

These moments were precious to both Maria and Amanda. It seemed that they hadn't had a chance to speak in ages. Their careers and the new families had pulled them apart. It felt good to rekindle their friendship. It was getting late, and both had to work the next day, but the time didn't seem to matter. One night is not much to give up for a childhood best friend.

Amanda inquired about Maria's job. She wanted to know all about the students she worked with and the community she worked in. Maria, of course was more than happy to discuss this issue with her. Maria described the South Bronx and the living conditions there. She told Amanda how she had never seen such poverty. The children that she worked with didn't have little things that they had taken for granted when they were children. Some had never owned a toy of their own. If the parents could afford toys, several children in the family would have to share one toy. Most of her students couldn't afford a small box of crayons containing only eight crayons. Maria often bought little things for her students such as pencils, notebooks, crayons, and even backpacks. She was happy to do it. She worked with the younger children who required Special Education.

Amanda asked how these children were diagnosed and who made the determination. She wanted to know who placed these children in special classes at such a young age. Maria explained that if they were below five years old, they were referred to by their pediatricians or their pre-school programs. Then they were evaluated by the Committee on Special Education in the district in which they lived.

"Remember when Elaine had so many problems learning?" asked Maria.

"Yes. We always helped her, so it wasn't so bad for her." answered Amanda.

"Elaine is learning disabled." stated Maria truthfully.

"What?" asked Amanda with genuine surprise.

"She is perfectly normal for everything. She just has trouble learning from books. That's what a learning disability is. Most of my students are learning disabled. I have some who are mildly mentally retarded and some who are Speech Impaired, but most of them are learning disabled." explained Maria.

"Too bad Elaine's parents didn't know about those special programs. Maybe Elaine would have done better in school with the appropriate help." said Amanda.

"She would have done better in school, but we wouldn't have met her. We wouldn't have had her treasured friendship." said Maria.

"God knows what he does." said both women together.

It was really getting late. Darkness had descended over Central Park, and all was quiet outside. No longer could the voices of pedestrians be heard from Amanda's porch. Maria and Orlando had not meant to stay so long. Angie had fallen asleep on the sofa in the living room and Orlando was dozing off in the den. Maria woke up her family and hugged Amanda warmly. This had indeed been a good evening.

Dona Angelica faces critical illness.

When the Rodriguez family arrived at their house, Dona Angelica met them at the door. There was a mystical look in her eyes. She stood on the front porch and stared first at Maria and then at Orlando.

"What do you want? she blared.

"What are you doing here?" she continued in the same tone of voice.

Maria and Orlando stood there incredulously. They couldn't believe what they were hearing. Dona Angelica grabbed Angie and took her to her room. Maria followed her.

"Mom, what's going on? How could you scream at Orlando and me like that? asked Maria.

"What are you doing in my house? What were you doing with my granddaughter? asked Dona Angelica with a scary sincerity.

"Mom, for God's sake. I am your daughter." said Maria, not understanding any of this.

"You are not my daughter. I never had any children." said Dona Angelica genuinely.

"Mom, if you never had children, how could you have a granddaughter?" asked Maria.

At that moment, Orlando appeared at the door of Angie's room. He took Maria by the hand and led her to their room. She held on to him feeling safe in his arms.

"There's no point in arguing with your mother. I think she has Alzheimer's disease." said Orlando.

"No." said Maria. "I can't accept that."

"We'll get a medical evaluation. In the meantime, be as nice as you can." suggested Orlando.

Maria went to sleep sadly. She was distressed at what she had heard her mother say. Maria tossed and turned all night thinking about her mom's possible illness. How could something like this happen? How could a woman who was always so hard working and productive not even know who her daughter is? No matter what happened Maria would always be there for Dona Angelica. She would take care of her.

Maria arrived at school late the next day. Usually, she took Angie to school and left Dona Angelica to wait for the home attendant by herself. She knew that she could no longer do that. She waited until the home attendant arrived and advised her of the occurrence the night before. She told her not to let Dona Angelica out by herself under any circumstances.

"Are you sick, Mrs. Rodriguez?" asked Jackie, one of Maria's students. "No. Why do you ask?" said Maria.

"You look so tired." said Jackie.

"Yeah, you look tired." added Juan, another student.

"If you are sick, maybe you don't want to give us homework." said Jackie.

"If you don't give us homework, you don't have to mark it." said Juan.

"Then you'll feel better. You'll feel like smiling. "Belkys chimed in.

This made Maria beam. It was so nice of her students to ask. They were only babies themselves. She knew that if she didn't give homework, it would make her students chuckle. But still it was very sweet of them to care enough to ask about her well-being. Looking at them, she remembered why she was a teacher. She laughed and went on with the class.

Maria went to work worried every day. She called home as soon as she arrived at the school and during her lunch hours. She made an appointment with her family doctor to look at her mother. The family doctor requested a CAT scans. The exam was inclusive. But Maria already knew what was wrong. She now had another challenge.

Orlando surprisingly was very cooperative. He drove Dona Angelica to all of her doctor's appointments. He gave the home attendants big tips to stay longer when he and Maria were going to be late. Orlando went out of his way to be kind and considerate of his mother-in-law. Maria didn't realize or didn't want to realize it, but Orlando knew that a patient with Alzheimer's disease didn't last long. He wondered how he would deal with Maria if Dona Angelica passed away. Maria had no brothers or sisters and no aunts and uncles. Dona Angelica was all she had.

Amanda's Suspicions

After her friends visited, Amanda felt good after her dinner party with Maria, Elaine, and their families. They had brought her back to her roots. Although she worked with poor children every day, she was paid good money and lived in a penthouse with her husband who was a millionaire. His practice was so much more lucrative than hers.

Maria and Elaine remained much closer to the community from which they all came. Spiritually and emotionally, they were much wealthier than she was. She never realized how much she had missed them.

Amanda began to work even harder at the clinic. After her talk with Maria about children born with handicapping conditions, she began to look more earnestly at her young patients. She began to ask the parents more questions about the children's developmental milestones. Amanda also began to research what agencies in the community could provide services such as Speech therapy, Physical therapy, and Occupational therapy to parents with Medicaid insurance or at reasonable prices. In one evening, her whole outlook was changing. There was more she could do for children besides medical treatment.

She saw less and less of Harold. They lived together but both worked long hours. Amanda began to wonder why Harold was at his office so much. His patients were wealthier than hers, but her clientele was so much larger than his. They both still served in the same hospital for emergencies.

Amanda didn't know if she was imagining things, but she felt that some of the staff were looking at her in an unusual manner. She thought that some of the people there were talking about her, and she couldn't understand why. Amanda had never been one to care about other people's opinions, so she was able to ignore this situation to a certain extent.

Harold began to go to his office even on Amanda's days off. Prior to the birth of the baby, Harold and Amanda always arranged to spend their free time together.

Amanda and Harold end their marriage

One day, Amanda was home with the baby. A woman called and asked for Harold. She must have noticed a trace of a Spanish accent in Amanda's voice and asked Amanda if she was the housekeeper. Amanda replied that she was Dr. Martinez-Fitzpatrick and that she was Dr. Fitzpatrick's wife. She informed the caller that this was Dr. Fitzpatrick's home number. The woman replied that she knew it was the home number. She declined to give her name when Amanda asked and hung up abruptly.

Amanda, however, saw the number in the caller I.D. box. The name was Sullivan, M. Amanda had never suspected Harold of infidelity. She had always been faithful in her marriage even when she and Harold disagreed and didn't talk to each other. She was loyal no matter how many hours each of them worked and no matter how much time they spent apart.

Amanda became pensive. For the first time, she began to distrust Harold. His parents had never come to meet her or their grandson. She had lived with that pain, but she gave Harold a lot of credit too. He married her despite his parents' opposition. Amanda always thought that he loved her so much that he defied his parents for her. Amanda was not jealous by nature. She had grown up in a Christian household. When all her friends went to private and parochial schools, she was saddened but she was not resentful.

This was different. The only man she had ever loved might be cheating on her. He had betrayed their commitment. Amanda started to feel faint.

Nothing had ever hurt so bad. But Amanda was a woman of science and she had always been logical. Maybe she should speak to Harold first. Maybe she should do some research and get the facts. She wasn't going to destroy her marriage on a whim or a falsity. But somehow, she knew what was to come. Her head told her to be logical, but her heart told her the truth.

Amanda dressed the baby and placed him in his lightweight stroller. She went downstairs and asked the doorman to hail a taxi for her. Amanda and the baby went to Harold's office which was just across town. She didn't walk because she'd have to go through Central Park with the baby. When she arrived, Harold's medical assistant told her that he was not there. She gave Amanda an incredulous look and said that it was his day off.

Now Amanda was sure. How could she have been so blind? She should have noticed Harold becoming more distant. She should have noticed his dearth of interest in the baby; she should have seen his lack of enthusiasm when she informed him about the baby. But the baby was a blessing from God and Amanda's life was forever wrapped around his. Harold might remain a part of their lives or not. Either way, the baby was her pride and joy. All her love was invested in him.

Amanda left the office and returned to her home. She called her mother from there and confided to her what was going on. She discussed her suspicions with her. She described to her the woman's call and Harold not being at the office. Well, Dona Lourdes wasn't going to just sit there while her daughter suffered. She grabbed her coat and hurried to the subway. Within the hour, she was sitting at Amanda's side.

"I am so sorry. I never liked the guy even if he was a doctor. There was just something about him." said Dona Lourdes.

"I have been so stupid. He seemed to be losing interest almost since the baby was born. I was so wrapped up in my work that I couldn't visualize what was taking place." said Amanda in a sorrowful tone.

"Don't you blame yourself for any of this. You are the victim here. You did nothing wrong. He has done everything wrong. He is not even a man. He is a low life." Dona Lourdes comforted her daughter.

Dona Lourdes took charge of the baby. She told the maid to go home early. She prepared dinner. She bathed the baby and put him to bed. Then she and Amanda relaxed in the living room. Harold appeared very late that night. He greeted Amanda as he walked in and held out his hand to Dona Lourdes. Dona Lourdes did not extend her hand in return.

"What's the matter, Mrs. Martinez?" inquired Harold, innocently.

"How was your day at work, Harold? Did you have many patients?" asked Amanda.

"Oh, yeah. You wouldn't believe how many. I finished just now." answered Harold.

"That's good considering you didn't go to the office." responded Amanda.

"What? Don't be silly. I was there all day." lied Harold.

"Well, you weren't there when I arrived with the baby. I went to tell you that Ms. M. Sullivan called here looking for you. Were you late to your rendezvous with her?" asked Amanda, too exhausted to sound angry.

Harold's mouth dropped open. He looked whiter than he normally did. Dona Lourdes glared at this hypocrite as her daughter challenged him with the facts. If he raised his voice or his hand, she would pounce on him. That's what mothers were for- to love and protect their children. Amanda was *her* baby.

"Well, so now you know. I should have told you. I guess I should have been truthful but I didn't know how. I don't want to elaborate on this in front of your mother. Honestly, I never meant to hurt you. This just happened." Harold finally told the truth.

"You just stop loving your wife and son." said Amanda.

"No, I wanted my son to look like me. I never thought of that when we married. After little Harold was born, I just didn't feel connected with him. He looks like you. He looks like your people. He looks like the Hispanic kids that I see in the park. You are beautiful but I guess my ego precludes me from loving my dark-skinned child. It's a feeling I just haven't been able to eradicate." Harold spoke truthfully, his every word wounding Amanda and infuriating her mother.

"You are a son of a bitch." screamed Dona Lourdes.

"That may be so, but now I am an honest one." responded Harold without feeling.

"Get your things and leave. I'll have my lawyer contact you regarding the divorce." ordered Amanda.

Harold left that night. He packed all his clothes and called a cab. He telephoned his parents and told them where to contact him. Afterwards, he left quietly. He didn't look at or ask about the baby who slept quietly in his room.

Amanda went back to work the next day trying to pretend that this was just a bad dream. She wanted to think that her husband was not cheating on her, and she was not on the verge of divorce. Emotionally she was drained. She felt weak for the first time in her life. This was a situation she had no control over. Besides, there was little Harold to think of. The baby was just about abandoned by his father. Amanda couldn't believe that Harold was embarrassed by the appearance of his own son. The baby was so beautiful; anyone would be proud to be his parent.

All the money she had earned, and her medical degree could not save her from this anguish. She would now be mother and father to her son. She'd own up to the responsibility. She knew that she could.

Amanda sought refuge in her old friends, Maria, Elaine, and Carmen. It occurred to her that throughout her life she had not made many associates. She went through high school and college and had not made any new acquaintances there. Thank God for the three best friends she met way back in first grade at St. Agatha's. Otherwise, she'd be all alone except for her parents.

It became known at the hospital that Dr. Fitzpatrick and Dr. Martinez-Fitzpatrick had separated. No one asked Amanda questions because she had not let any faculty members get close enough to her. M. Sullivan turned out to be a nurse who worked the same shift as Harold. This was no surprise.

Amanda vowed to get on with her life and her profession. There were many poor children out there in need of medical services and there was her son at home. Harold was out.

Dona Angelica develops a more serious illness.

"Hello." said Maria.

Is this Mrs. Rodriguez?" asked the voice at the other end.

"Yes, it is." answered Maria.

"Hi, this is Anna at the supermarket. The manager asked me to call you. Your mother was here. She walked down the aisle, took several cans of beans and other things, placed them in a bag herself and left. The man- ager said not to bother her." explained Anna.

"I'll be right there to pay for the groceries." said Maria.

When Maria arrived, she went directly to the manager's office. He told her what had happened and how he directed the security guard to watch her but not to say anything. Maria had already spoken to the local merchant about her mother's condition. Maria gave the manager her credit card and asked him to make an imprint. She told him to charge her card anytime Dona Angelica took something. Maria left with a heavy heart. Every day there was a new problem.

Amanda has a crisis.

"Hello" said Maria. It was 4 a.m. and it was a school day, so she didn't appreciate the phone ringing at this hour.

"Hello, hello, hello." said the voice sounding drunk or high on drugs.

"Who is this? How dare you call at this hour?" asked Maria, angrily.

"I'll call when I want. We're friends since the first grade." said the voice.

"Amanda?" asked Maria. "You're kidding. What's going on?"

Orlando was now awake and sitting up in bed. He was confused and annoyed at the caller. Maria looked over at him and told him she thought

Amanda was on the phone, and she sounded strange. This explanation made him more mixed up. He knew Amanda was a very stable person.

"Nothing. I just wanted to say goodbye. Today is my last day on earth." said Amanda.

"What?" asked Maria, really and truly worried.

"I decided to take an overdose of barbiturates. I remembered your phone number and I thought it was rude to not call and say farewell to my best friend." said Amanda, calmly.

"Wait!" yelled Maria. "I'm coming over. Don't take anything more.!"

Maria jumped out of bed. She threw her coat over her pajamas. She told Orlando she was going to Amanda's house. She told him Amanda was trying to commit suicide. Maria woke up Angie, who was nine years old, and told her to stay in her grandmother's room and not let grandma leave the house. The home attendant would be there at 7 a.m. Maria ran into the street and hailed a cab who drove her to Amanda's. Orlando called 911 from their house.

"I'm here to see Dr. Martinez Fitzpatrick." Maria told the doorman.

"That's not possible at this time, ma'am." responded the doorman.

"Yes, it is. This is an emergency." yelled Maria.

The doorman accompanied Maria on the elevator. Amanda wouldn't answer the door so one of the maintenance men was called to open it. Maria found Amanda on the sofa in the living room. At this point, she was incoherent. Maria held her in her arms.

"Don't you dare die on me, girl!" screeched Maria, as she tried to revive Amanda.

Amanda opened her eyes slightly. Several minutes later the paramedics arrived. Maria directed them to take Amanda to the nearest hospital not -the one she worked in. She didn't want Amanda to be embarrassed later.

Maria called her house and let Orlando know that she was going to the hospital with Amanda. Maria looked for the baby and didn't find him in his room. She asked Amanda and Amanda mumbled something about her mother. Maria called Dona Lourdes and was informed that the baby was with her. She told her what had happened and that she was taking Amanda to the hospital.

Maria sat in the waiting room remembering how she and Amanda had become friends. They sat together in class in first grade, and they had lunch together. They played in the school yard, and they played in the Gowanus Park. They had shared each other's joys and sorrows. Now Amanda might not survive the overdose she had taken. Maria wondered what had caused this decision on Amanda's part. She had a hard time with Harold's infidelity but she was very strong emotionally. If Amanda survived, they would talk. Orlando arrived in his car and Dona Lourdes came shortly afterwards. Amanda's father was home taking care of the baby. Maria thought Amanda must have planned this. She deliberately left the baby with her mother.

They sat in the waiting room for what appeared to be hours. No one wanted to talk. No one wanted to speculate as to what could have caused Amanda to do a thing like this. Maria called Elaine and Carmen and notified them about Amanda's affliction. Both wanted to help.

"I'm coming to New York immediately." said Carmen sounding distressed.

"I'm coming to the hospital now. I'm taking the day off from work." said Elaine.

Maria prayed silently and hoped with all her heart that she had gotten there on time. She was glad that Amanda, despite her condition, had called her. She felt that their friendship must be very potent. Elaine arrived within the hour with her daughter who is now eleven years old.

Eventually, the doctor came out to speak to them. Amanda was going to be just fine. She would have to stay in the hospital for at least two more days, but she had surely survived. The doctor said that they could go in to see Amanda two at a time and that they could not stay long. Family members could go first. Dona Lourdes and Maria went in first. Amanda's mother ran into the room and held her daughter in her arms as if she would never let go. Tears flowed down Maria's face.

"Why?" pleaded Maria.

"The divorce papers came today. I told Harold that I would divorce him, but I didn't even have time to see a lawyer yet. He must have been working on the divorce for a long time without saying anything to me. I signed the papers of course, but then I snapped. I felt so betrayed." explained Amanda.

"I'll get even with him. We'll take him for all he's worth." said the distraught mother.

"Mom. Don't worry. He left me the penthouse that is paid for and he's providing child support for the baby. He didn't, however, request visitation rights. He, without doubt, does not love that baby. He doesn't want to see him. I was devastated." said Amanda.

"You shouldn't have been. Medical degree or no medical degree, he's a monster. He's despicable. He was never good enough for you. We're here for you now. Forget him and go on with your life. A life that has been so productive" stated Maria.

Lourdes smiled at Maria's words. She felt gratified that Amanda had such a good friend. Her eyes watered as she thought about her daughter almost killing herself over such a worthless man. This should not have happened.

The nurse came to the door and asked that Maria and Dona Lourdes let the other visitors come in for a while. They stepped out and Elaine and Orlando went in to see Amanda. Elaine's eyes also filled with tears when she saw Amanda in her hospital bed. Amanda smiled weakly. After a short time, the nurse reappeared at the door and said that Amanda needed to rest. They could all return in the evening.

Carmen arrived at Maria's house late the next evening. Maria was just getting ready to visit Amanda again. Carmen had never been to Maria's house in Queens.

"So finally, I get to see your house." said Carmen.

"Finally. But you have always had an open invitation." answered Maria.

"I know. I just never got around to it. I haven't been coming to New York." responded Carmen.

"I'm so glad that you came. Amanda will be so happy to see you." said Maria honestly.

"I hope so. I hope that I can help in some way. I can't believe what that idiot has done to Amanda. I can't believe that she would take it so hard. She is well rid of him." said Carmen.

"She is definitely better off without him, but we've got to make her see that. Her son will be her source of joy. She can do without the jerk husband." Said Maria.

"I won't leave New York until I know she's okay. I took a leave from work for one week. I can extend it if necessary." informed Carmen.

Maria insisted that Carmen stay at her house for the week. She moved Angie in with her grandmother and prepared the room for Carmen. Carmen was touched by Maria's efforts to welcome her into her home. Angie did not seem to mind sharing with Dona Angelica. Carmen was surprised, however, that Dona Angelica didn't recognize her or even remember her.

"Don't worry. There are days when Mom doesn't know me either." informed Maria.

Maria and Carmen went off to see Amanda. Elaine was there when they arrived. All three went upstairs together. Amanda was sitting up in her bed having dinner. She looked good and she even managed a smile when she saw her friends. She thanked them all, especially Maria.

"It has taken this calamity to show me how valuable your friendship is." said Amanda.

"We've always been there for each other. We shared everything since we were children even our daydreams." said Elaine.

"So, we'll continue to share our lives with each other. I shouldn't have lost contact just because I moved to Boston." said Carmen.

"It's important that we always be there. That we are never too busy for each other." said Maria.

"Amanda, you'll walk out of this hospital and continue to be a great mother, doctor, and friend. Your patients need you and so do we. Don't ever do something like this again." implored Elaine.

Maria, Carmen, and Elaine went home feeling much better. They visited Amanda until she was discharged from the hospital. Once she was home, they called her every day for over a month. Carmen called from Boston. The girls from Bergen didn't want to let go of each other. They were rekindling an allegiance that made them all stronger.

Amanda did go back to work. With the help of Maria, her mother, and her other friends, she pulled the pieces back together emotionally. She was not going to kill herself because of a broken heart. So, the man she loved didn't love her. She could live with that. She'd have to for her son's sake. She took that overdose in a moment of passion. Thank God she thought of calling Maria. Somehow the number just came to her.

Amanda threw herself into her work with more devotion than before. She spent more quality time with her son. When she wasn't working, she was with him. Maria and Angie came over more often and Amanda also visited them in Queens. Maria's presence in her life also had a soothing effect. The baby grew more and more attached to his mother. When Harold was there, they'd go out sometimes and leave the baby with her mother. She didn't do that now. Amanda diverted all her love to him.

The months went by. Amanda's divorce was finalized. Her ties with Harold were forever broken. Amanda began to feel an inner peace. She had reconciled with the fact that he was out of her life. He transferred to another hospital probably because of her. This occurrence made her life easier at the hospital. Soon everyone forgot about him. No one ever mentioned him. It was as if he were never even there.

Amanda felt strong again. The parents of her patients loved her. They hugged her and gave her gifts for Mother's Day and Christmas. She was pleased.

Dona Angelica's Final Memories

"I came from Puerto Rico in 1929. I finished the eighth grade in Puerto Rico. I didn't go to high school because my mother didn't know that high school was free for everyone. My first job was in a Ronzoni macaroni factory. I was on my feet twelve hours a day. Although it was tiring, I loved to work. The money was needed in my home, and I was happy to help. But working in a macaroni factory was such a menial job. I wanted to do something better. I studied sewing at night and I loved it immediately. I learned quickly. It is easy to do something when you love what you are doing.

I worked in the garment industry in Manhattan for almost forty years. I married Estefano Abate. He works in the docks. He's a long shoreman. He seems to be late today. But he'll come soon.

All my life I have been very independent. I worked for myself and never asked anyone for anything. When Estefano and I married, we had a little girl. She must be playing outside now. She is very well behaved, and she always comes home on time.

Something funny seems to be happening here. I don't know what it is. Yesterday I went out walking. When I came back, two police officers were outside my house talking to this young woman. The young woman was crying. When I came in, she looked relieved. I don' t know what her problem is.

I always went to work on my own. I never drove so I was always very adept at taking public transportation. I know this whole city. There isn't any place in New York City I can't get to except Staten Island. But I never had any need to go to Staten Island.

There's something funny going on. I went to the supermarket the other day to shop for my family and everyone was looking at me. You'd think they never saw someone shopping before. I was in a hurry because my husband was coming home soon so I took the express line. The girl at the cashier started writing down the names of the items I purchased. What a boar! Honestly! Young people are so bad mannered nowadays.

Every time I go out there is someone following me. This older woman wears a white dress all the time. She looks like a nurse, but if she is a nurse she should be working in a hospital. Why is she following me around in my neighborhood? By the way, this isn't the neighborhood I am familiar with. The streets have different names.

Here comes the young woman again. Sometimes, she almost looks familiar. She has big, beautiful eyes which are always filled with sadness. She's always asking me if I need anything. That's nice of her of course, but I've always been very independent. I wonder what she wants now."

Angie listened to her grandmother speak and didn't interrupt. What could she say? There was no appropriate answer. She turned the television on to the HBO in Spanish channel so that Dona Angelica could see the movie dubbed in Spanish. Then she sat back to watch it with her in the room they now shared. Grandmother couldn't be left alone anymore. Sometimes she'd get up during the night and leave. She remembered her grandmother before she developed this horrendous mental disease. Regardless of her illness, Angie loved her grandmother after whom she was named. She listened to her ramble on and pretended to be following what she was saying.

Dona Angelica fell asleep during the movie. She was sitting up in her bed. Angie laid her down in her bed and placed the blanket over her. When Angie woke up, her grandmother was still sleeping. She was unable to wake her, so she called her mom. When Maria came upstairs and checked, her eyes filled with tears. She looked at Angie and explained that God had taken grandma to heaven in her slumber.

Dona Angelica's Funeral

"What is Alzheimer's?" shrieked Maria at the burial. "It destroys lives." Amanda and Elaine each held one of her arms as she stumbled. Orlando, Angie, and Carmen followed. After the final prayers, they helped Maria back into the car. Maria was comforted by their warmth and concern.

She remembered her mother. Her mother was always there for her. Her mother who worked and sacrificed for her all her life. Dona Angelica exemplified everything that was good. The priest had said: "Sister Angelica has left us. She will no longer feel pain and sorrow. We are here to bear the burdens of this world. Now Maria bore the burdens of the world without her beloved mother."

The Girls of Bergen Street Reunite

Amanda's penthouse was certainly the right place to get together. This was the most beautiful place in New York. The housekeeper brought a tray of pastries and more coffee. The girls from Bergen Street had recounted most of the experiences in their lives.

Looking back into the chasms of their lives, they realized how lucky they were. Amanda was a doctor. She had a beautiful son on whom she lavished her affection. She had a thriving medical practice, and her patients adored her. She worked with love and enthusiasm. Her divorce from Harold confirmed that she did not need anyone to determine her self-worth.

Elaine had studied to be a licensed practical nurse. She worked in the hospital close to her home. She did not let her learning disability hold her back. Her work in the geriatric ward was very much appreciated by the elderly patients she took care of. Her husband, Domingo, had turned out to be an excellent husband and father. He ran a successful car repair business and his family lived well. They had a beautiful daughter named after Elaine's best friend, Carmen.

Maria accomplished her dream of becoming a teacher. She worked in the elementary school in the South Bronx for many years and had no plans of transferring. She was now a senior teacher and could transfer if she wanted to because she had a lot of precedence. Her husband, Orlando, was also a very good husband and father. He was not chosen for a major baseball team upon graduation from college, but he was a dedicated gym teacher who got along well with his students and colleagues.

Carmen became a very successful banker. She suffered a great deal of pain when her parents died in that tragic car accident. She was abruptly taken from the Ramos family and displaced to Boston. However, Carmen grew to love her aunt Mercedes and was happy with her. Although she was in a profession dedicated to making money, she showed a huge humanitarian spirit when she bought the apartment building in Jamaica Plain and saved its residents from eviction. This building had proven to be a good investment financially and spiritually. She came to New York right away when Amanda needed her help. She came when Dona Angelica died. Carmen had never married and never developed any intimate relationships. Still, she was happy.

They were best friends as children in Brooklyn attending St. Agatha's school and playing in the Gowanus Park. They had shared the most important parts of their lives with each other. Their children would be friends. However, the girls had realized something else with the most recent debacles. They understood that one of the most important assets that they had was their lifelong friendship. Amanda, Carmen, Elaine, and Maria looked at each other and looked forward to the rest of their lives-TOGETHER.

About the Author

Linda Prado Amnawah was born in New York City. She attended Barnard College, Columbia and received a bachelor's degree in Spanish and Education in 1976. She received two master's degrees from Teachers' College, Columbia University in 1977 and 1983. She has an administrative degree from Bank Street College of Education in 1993. She taught in the public school system in New York City from 1977 to 2016.